A WARNING . . .

By the time I reached the far side of the pool, Cheryl had been carried off in a current of bumper boats. I floored my accelerator and hit Alec from behind, sending him spinning around and bouncing off the side wall. It got his attention.

He bumped me, and before I knew it we were moving in a circle around the outer edge of the pool, bumping each other.

"So, how do you like our school?" I asked him.

"You came to the bumper boats to ask me about school?" he said, sideswiping me.

I came around, pinning him against the dock. "I came to tell you something you might be too busy to notice."

"I notice everything." He tried to squeeze his way past, but I stayed just in front of him, keeping him pushed up against the dock.

"You might not notice *this*." I leaned forward, getting as close to him as I could, and said as quietly as I could under the circumstances. "You need to watch yourself," I told him. "Because there are some people who aren't too happy with your success. I just felt I should warn you."

Then his face hardened as he looked at me. "Are you threatening me?"

■ ■ ■

"The author deftly narrates a suspenseful story. . . the plot moves along quickly and sustains the tension until the last page. Hard to imagine it being any better written."

—VOYA

OTHER SPEAK BOOKS

THE
SHADOW
CLUB
RISING

NEAL SHUSTERMAN

speak

An Imprint of Penguin Group (USA) Inc.

SPEAK
Published by Penguin Group
Penguin Group (USA) Inc.
345 Hudson Street, New York, New York 10014, U.S.A.
Penguin Books Ltd, 80 Strand, London WC2R ORL, England
Penguin Books Australia Ltd, 250 Camberwell Road,
Camberwell, Victoria 3124, Australia
Penguin Books Canada Ltd, 10 Alcorn Avenue, Toronto, Ontario, Canada
M4V 3B2
Penguin Books (N.Z.) Ltd, 182-190 Wairau Road, Auckland 10, New Zealand

First published in the United States of America by Dutton Children's Books,
a division of Penguin Putnam Books for Young Readers, 2002
Published by Speak Books, an imprint of Penguin Group (USA) Inc., 2003

10 9 8 7 6 5 4 3 2

THE LIBRARY OF CONGRESS HAS CATALOGED THE DUTTON EDITION AS FOLLOWS:
Shusterman, Neal.
The Shadow Club rising / by Neal Shusterman.—1st ed.
p.   cm.
Sequel to: The Shadow Club
Summary: Even though he has disbanded his Shadow Club, formed to play
mean-spirited tricks on his enemies, fourteen-year-old Jared finds himself sus-
pected when a popular boy at school becomes the target of new pranks.
ISBN 0-525-46835-8
[1. Practical jokes—Fiction. 2. Clubs—Fiction. 3. Schools—Fiction.] I. Title.
PZ7.S55987 Sj 2002   [Fic]—dc21 2001045206

Speak ISBN 0-14-250089-5

Printed in the United States of America

For Erin Dayne

ACKNOWLEDGMENTS

The Shadow Club would not have risen had it not been for the following intrepid individuals, whose support and encouragement paved the way for this book: Dr. Steve Layne, whose passion for *The Shadow Club* convinced me that it deserved a sequel; Stephanie Owens-Lurie, whose support and editorial wisdom has been a guiding light throughout my career; Kathleen Doherty, who first rescued the Shadow Club and saw the potential for a sequel; Frank Hodge, whose dedication to children's literature has touched thousands of hearts from coast to coast; Jeff Sampson, David Ruskey, Rachel Morgan-Wall, and all my other on-line fans, whose ideas and enthusiasm continue to inspire me :); and Dr. Donald Levy, for his friendship and expertise on allergic reactions. And my children, Brendan, Jarrod, Joelle, and Erin, who are a critical audience for all my first drafts and a constant source of joy and inspiration.

THE
SHADOW
CLUB
RISING

Prologue

THE SEA AND I have never been friends.

We're more like neighbors who nod politely in passing while keeping a respectful distance. There was a time when the sea and I battled. It was a night lit by the flames of a burning lighthouse, when the surf was charged with an off-shore storm. It was the moment of my greatest triumph, and my deepest failure—triumph because I beat the sea, cheated death, and saved a kid's life; failure because I finally had to admit my guilt for every awful thing the Shadow Club had done. It wasn't just admitting it to others, I had to admit it to myself. If you know what happened—and you probably do, since it's no secret in this town—then you already have your own opinion of me. If you don't know about it, well, all the better, because maybe you won't judge me before you get to know me.

There are times now when I'm drawn to thoughts of what happened. When my mind is quiet, I start thinking about that day. I have this shiny seashell, about the size of my fist, that I found on the beach when I was little. Sometimes I'll lie on my bed and toss it up and down, fidgeting with it while I think about things I should probably try to forget. They say you can hear the ocean in the spirals of a seashell, and I used to believe it with all my heart. But now, of course, I know it's just echoes of the world around you, caught in the twisting spiral. Which maybe explains why I *do* hear the ocean when I put my ear to the seashell these days. Not just the ocean, but the roar of the flames from that burning lighthouse—two things still caught in the spiral, echoing round and round in my own world.

That's the way it was with the Shadow Club. We thought it was all over, but it had only just begun. The fires, the war against Tyson McGaw, all the dark and dastardly pranks—they were nothing compared to what happened next. In the end we had all confessed to the things we had done—we thought that by purging ourselves of the guilt, it would all just go away. Of course we knew we'd have to pay for the things we did, but even then there was relief in knowing that once we paid our debts to society, we could gather up our lives again and move beyond it. But anger and hatred and resentment—those feelings are as slippery as a greased pig: hard to handle, and even harder to catch when they get loose. Feelings like that don't die easily—they just move on to other people if they can't have their way with you.

Like I said, we'd thought it was over, until February, when everything crept up on us, slamming into us from behind like a traffic accident.

It started, like so many things in my life seemed to have started, with Austin Pace. But this time things were a whole lot different. . . .

The Iron Maiden

I HAVE A BIKE, but I don't ride it much. In our town there are too many hills, and the roads aren't paved as well as they should be. The shoulders are littered with rocks broken loose by the rains and the roots of tall pines. I've always relied on my feet to get me places. In the mornings I run to school, even in the winter, when my nose and ears grow so cold that they feel numb all through first period.

Now that I was officially off the track team, all that running I did to get from place to place meant a whole lot more to me. But on this particular day I didn't run, I walked, because I wasn't in a hurry to get to this destination.

It was the middle of January. Cold to me, but then nowhere near the deep freeze that other parts of the country got. While other places were getting blizzards, we'd just get rain, and when snow did fall it never lasted. The only white Christmas we ever see is from the fog that rolls in from the ocean.

It was getting dark as I walked along the winding, tree-lined road that led to the homes on the hill. My social studies teacher said that in Third World countries the higher up you are on the hill, the poorer you are, because it means that you don't have any water or electricity. But not so in the world I live in. The homes up the hill have pools and big yards and picture windows with million-dollar views. Austin Pace lived about two-thirds up. Not high enough to be in a mansion, but high enough to be able to look down his nose at two-thirds of the rest of us, which he had always done quite well.

Three months ago I had been indirectly responsible for breaking his ankle—and now I was going to his house for dinner. I had to admit I couldn't have come up with a worse punishment myself. I kept reminding myself that I wasn't *actually* the one who spread those sharp rocks on the field—rocks that cut up his bare feet and mangled his right ankle. *That* had been Cheryl Gannett—my life-long friend and now ex-girlfriend. She had done it for me without my knowledge or consent to get Austin back for all the nasty things he had done to me. She did it because I was the second-best runner—all the members of the Shadow Club were second best at something. I had to admit that none of the indignities he had made me suffer came close to the vicious games the Shadow Club had played. Austin had once apologized for treating me the way he had. That was in the nurse's office, after I carried him off the field. He reneged on his apology later, though, when he found out I was partially to blame for his injury. "Pain makes people delirious," he said, and claimed he hadn't meant a word of it.

So then why was I being invited to dinner? I asked myself. Had Austin finally accepted my apology? Or was it because my parents paid his uncovered medical expenses with the money they had set aside for buying me a car in a couple of years? Maybe he felt bad because I had resigned from the track team as part of my penance for the Shadow Club's deeds. Or maybe, I thought, he invited me over to dinner just to poison me.

And so I walked instead of ran.

"Oh, it's you," said Allison, Austin's younger sister, as she opened the door. She said it with such contempt, it was clear she had been practicing saying that for most of the day.

"Come in, Jared," said Mrs. Pace, with a smile that was way too inviting. Her husband sat in the background, reading in an armchair—but the moment I stepped over the threshold, he quickly folded his newspaper and went into the other room. Austin was nowhere to be seen.

"Please, make yourself at home," Mrs. Pace said. There was enough brightness in her voice to light up the Astrodome.

This is all too weird, I wanted to say. *Can I go now?* But instead I just said, "Sure." And I sat down, trying to look comfortable, even though I felt as if I were sitting on a bed of nails.

"We're having pot roast," Mrs. Pace said cheerfully. "You eat meat, don't you?"

"He probably eats it raw," said Allison.

Austin came downstairs, slowly hobbling. The truth was, he had been walking just fine for the past few weeks, but whenever he saw me, his limp mysteriously returned. That was okay. After what the Shadow Club had done to him, if he wanted to rub salt in my guilt, he had every right to do it, so I played along.

"Still hurts?" I asked.

"Only when I move."

I offered a slim smile, but I couldn't hide just how uneasy I was about this whole dinner. He seemed to take some comfort in my discomfort. I stood up, putting out my hand to shake, knowing that he wouldn't take it. Seeing me put down my hand unshaken seemed another moment of satisfaction for him.

"I want you to know," he said, "that this wasn't my idea. It was my mother's."

The dining table was set for five, but only four sat down when dinner was served. Mr. Pace did not join us—although I could hear newspaper pages turning in another room.

As Mrs. Pace brought out the serving dishes, I found myself grabbing the food far too quickly—not because I was hungry, but because I wanted to occupy my mouth with chewing, so I wouldn't be forced to talk. Austin seemed to have the same idea, but his sister had different plans.

"So," Allison asked, "what was it like being suspended?"

I looked down at my plate, wishing the meat was a little tougher so I could continue to chew for a few minutes without having to speak. "It gave me a lot of time to think," I answered.

"I thought you had to have a brain for that," Austin said.

"Now, Austin," his mother said, "Jared's our guest tonight."

"So you keep telling me."

The newspaper turned in the other room.

Finally I broke down and asked the question that had been plaguing me since I had received this invitation. "I hope you don't mind me asking, Mrs. Pace, but . . . why am I here?"

"For dinner, of course," she said.

It was Austin who explained. "The self-help book my mom's been reading says we have to make peace with all the people we hate."

"And," added Allison, "there's nobody we hate more than you."

"More string beans, Jared?" asked Mrs. Pace.

Back in seventh grade I did a report on medieval torture

techniques; people stretched on the rack, or made to stand in the dagger-lined shell of the Iron Maiden. I should have included "Dinner With the Paces" in my report.

I continued to stare into my food, moving my fork around and around until the potatoes became a brown sludge lagoon beside my island of meat.

"Listen," I said, unable to meet their eyes, "the Shadow Club was a mistake. What we did was wrong. And I'm sorry."

"You're sorry?" said a man's voice behind me. I turned around to see Mr. Pace standing at the threshold of the dining room. "You think that ruined ankle and the scars on Austin's feet will go away just because you say you're sorry?"

"No," I said, forcing myself to look him in the face, no matter how small it made me feel. "But I'm sorry anyway."

After he left the room I could still feel his eyes on me.

"I've lost my appetite," said Austin, dropping his fork on the plate with a clatter. Then he stormed away, remembering his limp halfway out of the room, leaving me to be killed by his mother's kindness.

I ate quickly, said a polite thank-you, and headed for the door—but even as I did, I knew that I couldn't leave like that. I knew I had to say something to Austin, though I didn't know what it would be. I found him in his garage, which had been converted into a game room, playing pool by himself.

"You're still here?" he said, shooting at the nine ball and missing completely. Either he wasn't very good, or my presence was throwing his game off. "What is it you want?"

I took a deep breath and spoke, not sure what I would say until the words came tripping out of my mouth. "I stepped down from the track team, I've apologized a thousand times, but it doesn't seem to make a difference. What is it going to take to even up the score between me and you? I want to know what I can do to make you happy, because whatever it is, I want to do it. I owe that to you."

Austin put his cue stick down. "You can't stand the fact that I hate your guts, can you?"

"I guess you have every reason to hate me," I admitted. "Me, Cheryl, Randall, and the others."

Then Austin took a step closer, and said, "Then let me hate you . . . because that's what makes me happy."

"How was dinner with the Paces?" my dad asked when I got home.

"Fine," I said. It was a one-word response that said nothing. Things were like that between me and my parents these days. Although I had always been able to talk to them before, ever since the disaster at the lighthouse, there was like this no-fly zone between us, and we really couldn't talk the way we used to. It was as if they didn't quite see me when they looked at me now. I don't know what they saw. It's very unsettling not to be able to see yourself reflected in your own parents' eyes, if you know what I mean.

"Just fine?" my dad said, pressing me for info.

"Yeah. Fine."

He opened the refrigerator like he wanted something to eat, but he was just pretending so that he didn't have to look at me. I knew that trick, because I often did it myself.

"Everything okay at school?"

"You mean aside from the casualties from the elephant stampede?"

Now he stared at me with one hand on the open refrigerator door.

"I'm kidding, Dad."

He shut the door. "You have your mother's sense of humor."

Funny, because Mom always accused me of having *his* sense of humor. Lately neither of them would take credit for me.

As I went to my room, I began to think about the ex-members of the Shadow Club. Cheryl, who had taken my offhand comment about forming a club for second-best kids and turned it into reality; her younger brother, Randall, who had always been hundredths of a second away from first place on every swim team he'd ever been on; Darren Collins, who never saw the glory he deserved in basketball; Jason Perez, whose dreams revolved around a trumpet solo he'd never been asked to perform; Karin "O. P." Han, who was always One Point away from having the highest grades in school. Abbie Singer, who was almost, but not quite, the most popular girl around. And then, of course, me—the king of the silver medal in the hundred-yard dash.

It all seemed so important just a few months ago, but when you terrorize your enemies the way we did, you lose your taste for blood—and although I still had the urge to be better at what I did, I no longer had the need to be better *than*.

It all came down to this: I could deal with myself now. I had come to terms with the things we had done . . . but that look of hatred on Austin's face—that was something I still couldn't deal with.

"Do you hate me, Tyson?" I asked from the threshold of his room that night. It used to be our guest room, but now Tyson was a permanent guest.

He didn't answer my question. Instead he held up the drawing he was working on. "How do you like this one?" he asked. It was an intricate pencil sketch of a city skyline.

"I like it," I said with a sly smile. "It's not on fire."

"Ha-ha," he said. I think I was the only person who could joke with him about that—perhaps because I had been there during the last blaze he had set, when he burned down his house and nearly took both of us with it. I don't take blame for everything in the world, but a good part of that was my fault, too, because I was really the one who had pushed Tyson to do it.

I took a look at the drawing. It was good—all his artwork was good—and, like I said, the fact that he didn't draw anything burning was a good sign. So many of his sketches and paintings had everything from airplanes to buildings to people being consumed by flames. His psychiatrist said it was good for him to air his demons through his artwork, but it still didn't make it any less creepy.

How Tyson ended up with my family is something I can take a little bit of pride in. After his lighthouse burned and I rescued him from drowning in the ocean, he had been taken away from his foster parents. They were the third ones he had lived with since his real parents died when he was just a little kid. With no one else willing to take him, he would have been stuck in Pleasant Haven Children's Home, which was neither pleasant nor much of a haven—it was just a last-stop orphanage with a deceptive name. I was the one who insisted that we take him in—that *we* become his new foster family. Although my parents were definitely not too keen on the idea of an angry pyromaniac kid in the house, they knew I owed him even more than I owed Austin. In spite of the history between Tyson and me, even Social Services agreed that placing him with us was better than sending him to Pleasant Haven. When I was younger I always kind of wanted a brother. Of course Tyson wasn't what I'd had in mind, but I sort of liked it.

Tyson turned a page in his sketch pad and started a new drawing, forgetting, or pretending to forget the question I had asked when I first stepped in.

"So, Tyson," I said once more, refusing to let him off the hook, "do you hate me?"

He shifted uncomfortably. "Yeah, sure," he said. "Maybe a little."

"Maybe a lot?" I pushed.

"I don't know," Tyson answered. "Somewhere between a little and a lot—but closer to a little—and anyway, I wouldn't have come to live here if I didn't like you more than I hated you."

I smiled. "You can't stand me when I drag you out of your room in the middle of the night." Tyson grunted like a bull. Part of my penance, as far as Tyson was concerned, was setting my alarm for 1:00 and 4:00 A.M., then hauling Tyson out of bed to take a leak, with the hope of breaking that nasty little bed-wetting habit of his, which I had so thoroughly announced to the entire school.

"How do you deal with it when people totally hate your guts?" I asked.

"Very badly," he answered, and I realized what a stupid question that was to ask him—a kid who always went ballistic at the drop of a hat. "Is this about Austin?" he asked, knowing where I had gone to dinner that night.

I nodded. "I thought he might give me time off for good behavior, you know?"

"More like life with no chance of parole?"

"No," I said, "more like death row."

And then Tyson said something that I'll never forget.

"Sometimes people see you the way they want to see you," he told me, "no matter how hard you try to change it. It's like they'd rather twist the whole world just so they can keep seeing you the same lousy way."

It wasn't long until I knew how true that really was.

Alec Smartz

THE LETHAL BREW that the Shadow Club had set to simmer would have boiled over eventually, no matter what anyone did—I'm convinced of that—but it was the arrival of a certain person in town that really turned up the heat.

When some kids move into a new neighborhood, they make no ripple at all. They just slip into the back of the classroom while no one's looking, or simply replace someone else who just moved away. Then there's the kid whose entrance is like a cannonball jump into a still pool. Alec Emery Smartz Jr. was that kid.

Alec was slim, good-looking, and entered school on the top level, socially, academically, and even athletically. Although he wasn't the tallest kid in school, something about him gave you the impression that he was. He rode into our school in a mythical kind of way and quickly became legend.

Now, just to be clear on this, I had no problems with

Alec. Well, maybe just a little one when it came to him and Cheryl—but I'll get to that.

I first saw him in the office while I was filling out a tardy slip, because, well, punctuality has never been my strongest point. Alec was having a conversation with Principal Diller like they were golf buddies or something. Principal Diller asked if there were any extracurricular activities he might be interested in, and Alec responded in an "aw shucks" kind of way, saying, "I don't know—there are lots of things I like to do."

"Well, I'm sure you'll make a lot of friends here," Principal Diller said. Then he caught a glimpse of me and made sure Alec walked in the other direction. I pretended like that didn't bother me.

From that first time I saw him, I sensed Alec would be the epicenter of seismic activity in our school. It was the way he held himself, and the way he looked at you. Like he already belonged, before even making an effort. And then there was the name—"Alec Smartz." It was one of those cruel parental jokes that would be an eternal mystery. But then on the other hand, it was so obvious that only a moron would try to take advantage of it. Whenever some kid tried to call him "Smart Alec," he would say in a total deadpan, "Gee, that's clever. Nobody ever thought of that before," making the moron feel even more stupid than he was before, if that was possible.

But I guess, in a way, Alec Smartz was condemned to be

what he was, the same way so many people became slaves to their name—like our music teacher, Mr. Musiker, and the guy who runs the fruit stand down on Pine Street, Mr. Groesser.

It was a few days after dinner at the Paces that I made a point of meeting Alec rather than just see him brush past, or hear people whisper about him. I wasn't quite sure what the whispers were about, but I was getting more and more curious.

It was one of those rare mornings when I was actually on time. He and Cheryl were locking up their bikes. Apparently Cheryl had forgotten her lock at home, so Alec was chaining both of theirs together. I'd be lying if I said it didn't make me a little bit uncomfortable. He and Cheryl had been spotted together on several occasions since his arrival in town.

"Hi, Cheryl," I said, which was pretty much the limit of our conversations these days. Cheryl and I had been best friends for most of our lives, and for a short time we were more than friends, but now, well, I didn't know what we were. Accomplices, maybe. Co-conspirators. I missed our friendship but had no clue how to get it back.

"Hi, Jared," she said in a strained sort of way. "Have you met Alec?"

He shook my hand. "Nice to meet you."

"Yeah."

He was much friendlier than I had imagined he would be, but I should have guessed that—after all, Cheryl would never hang out with a creep.

"I hear you're a runner," he said.

"Was."

"Still are," said Cheryl. "He's just not on the team this year, that's all."

I offered no further explanation.

"Maybe we could go jogging sometime," Alec suggested.

"Jared doesn't jog—he runs."

Alec glanced toward the school. "Listen, I gotta go—the soccer coach wants to talk to me before class. It was nice meeting you." And off he went with a confidence that divided the packs of kids in his way.

I turned to Cheryl, wearing a smug little grin.

"Don't look at me like that," she said.

"Like what?"

"Like you know something." Cheryl checked her kickstand. "And anyway, I can be friends with anyone I want."

I had to laugh. "I didn't say anything about you and Alec!"

"But you were thinking it."

"Then you need more practice at reading minds."

Cheryl blew into her hands to warm them, and now that I had caught my breath from the long run to school, I was beginning to feel cold myself.

"So what do you think of Alec?" she asked.

"I think he's OK."

"Everyone likes him."

"He seems like a likable guy."

The first bell rang, and Cheryl turned to hurry into school, having never been tardy in her whole life.

"Cheryl," I called to her before she got to the school steps. When she turned, I said, "I think you two look good together."

She gave me her famous prosecutor's gaze, ready to deny that they were "together" at all, but instead she just said, "Thanks," and went inside.

I had to admit I wasn't lying. I thought they really did make a nice couple—and it really ticked me off.

Our school's just a block away from Pine Street—which was unfortunately the only street in town where all the pine trees had been cut down and replaced by sycamores. The street was lined with shops and cafés that had died when the mall opened up a few miles away, and then were reborn when people decided malls were boring and quaint little street shops were cool.

Among the various cafés was Solerno's Pizzeria, a place run by an old grimace of man whose taste buds must have been removed, because his pizza had more salt than the ocean, and enough garlic to keep the town free of vampires. Still, when compared to the school cafeteria, Solerno's was a world-class restaurant, and so kids flocked there during lunch, hoping for a thick slice of god-awful pizza, and hoping to catch miserable old Solerno in a less awful mood than usual.

That same afternoon, I ran into Alec and Cheryl at Solerno's during lunch. Alec was actually talking to the old man, suggesting that he change his selection of spices. I have to tell you, I would have laid down and worshiped Alec myself if he got through to Solerno, but, true to form, the old man threatened to hit him with a broom.

Still curious as to what made Alec tick, I sat down with him and Cheryl, and we suffered through our pizza together.

The conversation didn't go much of anywhere, until Cheryl decided it was time to get cute.

"Did you know Jared has a hidden talent?" she told Alec. "He can drink soda through his nose."

"Oh, c'mon, Cheryl, I haven't done that since fifth grade."

I have to admit, it was something I was once rather proud of—and although it always gave me one heck of a brain-freeze, it was worth it to impress friends and disgust adults, back when I was ten.

"Now *that's* something I'd like to see," said Alec. "I'll bet you can't do it anymore."

I don't know what came over me then. I guess I'm still a sucker when it comes to being challenged. So I took a deep breath, shoved my straw up my left nostril, pinched the right one closed, and began to guzzle. Drinking soda through your nose is like riding a bicycle—it's a skill you never quite forget. I downed the entire cup in fifteen seconds flat.

Cheryl laughed and applauded, and I felt . . . well . . . stupid for having actually done it.

"Cool," said Alec.

And that's when I thought I saw something change in him. The grin on his face was the same, but something about him suddenly shifted, and grew colder. Or maybe it was just my brain-freeze.

"I can do that," Alec said.

Cheryl laughed. "I wouldn't advise it. You should leave it to the professionals."

"No, really," Alec said, and before any of us knew it, he shoved his own straw up his right nostril—making me realize how completely asinine I must have looked—and began to drain his Dr Pepper into his face.

"Alec . . ."

It was a second before he gagged, coughing a spray of fizzing soda all over us. Some girls at the next table got spritzed; a guy behind us stood, fully prepared to give him the Heimlich; and from behind the counter, Solerno said, "You puke uppa my pizza, you don't getta no more!"

Alec quickly regained his composure, if not his dignity.

"Don't worry about it," I told him. "It takes years of hard work to master."

But he said, with a harshness hidden deep within his smile, "Practice makes perfect."

I looked at Cheryl, who just shrugged as if it were nothing, but somehow I knew better.

———

It only took a few days more until I knew all I needed to know about Alec Smartz. The stories circulating around school painted a whole gallery of pictures.

Painting number one: **Still Life With Algebra.**

Mr. Kronisch, our math teacher, gave bears of exams that were the subject of many a nightmare. For this reason his midterms were called the Kronisch Inquisition. Alec, being new, isn't expected to take the test, but he does anyway. He aces it, throwing the curve so far into orbit that everyone else's score goes down half a grade.

Portrait number two: **Self-portrait With Saxophone.**

While still scouting out the school those first few weeks, he wanders into Mr. Musiker's room during a mostly pathetic band rehearsal (which is no great surprise, since our band's rehearsals are always mostly pathetic).

"Do you play an instrument, Alec?" Mr. Musiker asks.

"A few," he responds, then proceeds to borrow Chelsea Morris's alto sax and plays a number that could get him a recording deal with the jazz label of his choice. You can almost hear the blood draining from all the wanna-be band stars in the room.

Portrait number three: **Alec at the Bat.**

Alec wanders innocently onto the baseball field—but by now I've come to realize that Alec doesn't really "wander" anywhere. All his casual arrivals are as well calculated as his answers on the Kronisch Inquisition. Today the baseball team is getting ready for the upcoming season.

"You interested in going out for baseball?" the coach asks.

"Well, it's not my sport," says Alec, "but I'll give it a try." Long story short, now there's a new shortstop, and a grin on the coach's face that has never been seen in all his years of coaching our losing baseball team.

When asked how he got so good, Alec says, "Nowhere in particular. I'm just good in any sport that involves a ball." It's a statement that makes all the coaches drool, and all the jocks run for cover.

When someone enters a school with as much noise as Alec did, emotions are bound to run high—in both directions.

"I don't like him," I heard Drew Landers, the star swimmer, say, obviously anticipating the day Alec Smartz "wandered innocently" up to the pool.

"I don't trust him," Tyson said, and for once Tyson's paranoia was reflected by many others.

"I heard he was a genetically engineered cyborg," said Ralphy Sherman, who had never uttered a word of truth in his life. And what was scary was that some kids believed him.

I had my own theory, however. Simply put, Alec Smartz was just plain *good*. It was the kind of "good" that was not locked into a specific sport or subject. Alec was one of those rare individuals whose talent was like a suitcase he could carry through anyone's door, whether it was the door to the music room, the math room, the gym, or even the door to a pizza place, where he inhaled a can of Dr Pepper through his nose one week after seeing me do it, breaking my twelve-ounce record by four seconds.

Whether he worked hard to be so good I couldn't quite say, but that didn't matter because he made it look easy. In fact, he seemed to get his jollies by making everything look so easy that the rest of the world looked bad.

Thanks to him, the entire school now qualified for membership in the Shadow Club.

Freaks Like Me

NOBODY SEES THEMSELVES as "the bad guy." Even the nastiest, most evil people are heroes in their own minds. I thought I was still a pretty good guy. In the past, whenever I had screwed up, people never got too bent out of shape. "Your heart's in the right place," they would always say, and that's how I still felt about myself. Even when my brain took an extended vacation, I could be forgiven, because my heart was in the right place. Of course the Shadow Club's victims would never believe that, but I just assumed that everyone else who knew me would. Sometimes it takes a good left hook to open your eyes.

The fight started as Tyson's—not mine. Although it was now harder for kids to whip Tyson into that fighting frenzy he was so famous for, it wasn't impossible. Those same kids who had always tormented him now worked overtime to make him nuts. Like Tyson said, people see you the way they want to see you . . . and sometimes they manage to turn you into the very thing they want to see.

It was just before lunch, when everyone was most irritable, that our school's designated nuisance, Brett Whatley, heaped one too many rude remarks on Tyson's head. By the time I happened by, they were already into it, swinging full force, and bouncing back and forth across the hall in a locker-bashing brawl. I have to admit, I seriously considered just walking the other way, and letting the fight take care of itself . . . but like I said, my heart was in the right place. See, if Tyson won the fight, he'd probably be suspended, and if he lost the fight, he'd be drawing pictures of things burning again. I couldn't let either one happen, and since no teacher arrived to break it up, I took it upon myself. I pushed my way through the chain of spectators, squeezing myself into Brett and Tyson's airspace, and taking a nasty elbow to the ribs from Tyson before he realized it was me.

"Back off!" I yelled at Tyson, loud enough to break through his anger.

"But . . . but he called me a—"

I turned to Brett, before Tyson could finish. "You want to fight someone, Brett, why don't you start with me?"

And for an instant Brett Whatley looked scared. The kid was practically a head taller than me. But here he was, backing away from me.

It only lasted a second, though, until he remembered that he had an audience.

"Well, if it isn't Jared Mercer," he sneered. "I should have known I'd find you holding Tyson's leash."

He couldn't even come up with an original insult. He stole that one from *Star Wars*.

"Why don't you get a life and lose it," I told him.

"You and Tyson deserve each other—you're both a couple of losers."

Although I thought I was immune to Brett Whatley's brainless taunts, they were starting to get to me.

"Just leave us alone."

He crossed his arms, sensing he had the upper hand. "Why? What are you gonna do, Mercer, put a bomb in my locker? Or maybe just a razor blade in my sandwich."

Hearing him say that knocked the wind right out of me. Those comments came so far out of nowhere that I thought I had somehow missed part of the conversation. "What?"

Then a voice from the sidelines chimed in as well. "Maybe he'll just break your kneecaps in your sleep."

And someone else said, "Or maybe he'll just kill your dog."

I looked at the faces of the kids around me. I couldn't tell who had spoken—but by the look of distrust on their faces, it could have been any of them. Some of them even backed away, as if I might actually do those things to *them*. These were kids I knew, kids I had studied with, played with, and joked with for years. Now they were kids I suddenly didn't know, or at least they didn't know me. Did they really believe I was capable of such awful things because I had been in the Shadow Club?

Brett sneered at me, sensing the support all around him.

"You know, there's a word for freaks like you," he said.

But whatever word he had in mind, no one was hearing it today, because I launched at him with both fists swinging. "I would never do those things!" I screamed as I fought him, making each word strike home with another wild punch. "I would never . . . never . . . never . . . never . . . never . . ." Finally Tyson pulled me away—*he* was the calm one trying to cool *me* down.

"Did you hear what he said?!" I screamed at Tyson. "Did you hear?!" I began to get furious at Tyson. How could he be so calm? And then someone else grabbed me, spinning me around. I was ready to fight with this new assailant as well . . . until I realized who it was. I was standing fist to face with our vice principal and guidance counselor—Mr. Greene.

Brett was sent to class.

Although *he* began the fight with Tyson—although everyone knew that Brett created every disaster he was involved in—he was let go, and I was brought in for disciplinary action. Me, alone.

The fury had left me by the time I landed in Mr. Greene's office. Now there was a knot in my gut that spread out through my whole body, as if my entire body was clenched like a fist.

"I can see you've made no effort to clean up your behavior," Mr. Greene said to me.

"So, I got into a fight—so?"

He said nothing.

"I mean, everyone fights once in a while," I added, "and I haven't done anything wrong for months!"

He swiveled calmly in his chair. "At least not that we know about."

"What's that supposed to mean?"

"It means that you played me for a fool once before, and I won't let it happen again."

It took a moment for me to process that.

"Kids like Brett Whatley are easy," he continued. "With Brett you always know exactly what you're getting. You know what fights he'll pick, what insults he'll throw. You know what he's going to do before he does it. He's predictable, and in my book that makes him pretty harmless."

I looked down at my shoes. "I don't think so."

"But you, Jared, you're not like that. When you pull something, you don't leave a trail behind you—there's no 'smoking gun.' You're quiet . . . and you're sneaky. In my book, that makes you dangerous."

It was all coming into focus now as he spoke: what he thought of me—how he saw me. The category he had me filed under. This wasn't about the fight, was it? The fight was just an excuse to bring me in—so he could read me this little riot act. It was as if these past three months had meant nothing. As if the only reason I hadn't been in trouble since then was that I simply hadn't been caught.

"Just because I'm quiet doesn't mean I'm sneaky."

"And just because you show remorse doesn't mean that you're really sorry for anything."

"I *am* sorry!"

"I wish I had a reason to believe that."

"You'll never have a reason!" I shouted at him. "Because you don't want to find one!"

He considered that and, for a moment, I could see him squirm a little. It was his job to peg kids, and he was good at what he did. So good that he would never accept being wrong. Whatever label he had chosen for me, he would fight to the death to make sure it stuck like a *kick me* sign tattooed to my butt.

"You don't know what's inside me," I said to him, feeling my eyes moisten, but I refused to be brought to tears.

"You're right, Jared, I don't," he said. "And that's what scares me."

Great Balls of Fur

IT TAKES EVERY ounce of your strength not to become what they make of you. Your spirit could implode under the pressure the way mine did that day with Brett . . . but in a way that opened my eyes, letting me see the trouble brewing around me—trouble that everyone else was blind to.

The Winter Carnival was a tradition in our town, started by a mayor too cheap to pay for a summer carnival. Since no one else wanted to throw a carnival in the dead of winter, we ended up with twice the rides at half the price for two whole weeks instead of just one. This year I got a weekend job at one of the carnival ticket booths to take my mind off things. You learn a lot working at a ticket booth. The conversations of people in line make you a local expert, because the ticket booth is a crossroads for all the town gossip. Who was getting married and who was likely to get divorced; who was cheating on his or her spouse and who was cheating the government. I learned so much about Alec Smartz that I could have written his biography. There were the kids who were impressed by him—younger kids mostly—seventh and eighth graders idolized him. There were the girls who vied for his attention and were endlessly irritated by the fact that Cheryl got most of it. And then there were the others. The ones who neither worshiped nor fawned. The ones who were not amused. *"The way he plays that saxophone you'd think he was born with it growing from his mouth,"* they would say, or *"What, does he have a homing beacon in his baseball mitt?"* It wasn't so much their words, but the way they said them— oozing with hatred. A girl whose name I didn't know talked to me as I sold her tickets, telling me how Alec became the overnight star of the chess team.

"He keeps stomping on you until you stop moving," she said. "He doesn't just beat you, he *squashes* you." And she was right. It was like anyone with any talent was a cockroach he had to crush. "Someone ought to do something about him," she said. "Someone ought to put him in his place."

Then she winked at me. "Of course, it would take more than one person to do it right," suggested the chess girl. "Make it so it would stick. It would take kids with *experience* in that sort of thing."

Now I realized why so many of the conversations about Alec were loudly spoken in my direction. *Someone ought to put him in his place.* More than one person had suggested that to me, and with it came the unspoken threat, *"If you don't, Jared, then we will."*

"Here are your tickets," I told her. "If you want more, go to the other booth across the park. Don't come back to me."

I saw Alec and Cheryl at the carnival that Sunday just before my shift ended. They had already been to the midway, because Alec was carrying around this huge blue giraffe he had won at one of the games. Although he could have left it somewhere, he made a point of lugging it around as he zigzagged through the carnival, in case there was anyone left who hadn't seen that he had won it. I imagined him sitting in his garage for weeks on end hurling footballs at tires, or tossing coins at little glass plates, so when it finally came time for the real event, he would do it in just one shot, making it look like anyone should have been able to do it. I was the one who noticed all the looks he got—the wide-eyed looks from those in his fan club, and the narrow-eyed glares from those who resented him.

When my shift was over I wandered through the fair, trying to convince myself that I really wasn't looking for Alec and Cheryl. His big stuffed giraffe was sitting propped up against the rail of the bumper boats. The line had already emptied out onto the semicircular dock of the bumper-boat pool. I hopped the rail and handed a few ride tickets to the attendant. He pointed me to one of the last available boats that actually worked, then started my engine with a pull cord, like a lawn mower.

Bumper-boat racing is more or less an individual sport. One person per boat, and everyone out for themselves. Even when you try to do it in teams, it's never long before your own teammates turn on you without warning. The little inner-tube boats began to bounce around like angry atoms in a mad scientist's brew, with everyone trying to keep away from the ice-water fountain in the center of the tank. You'd think someone would realize that getting drenched in the middle of winter wasn't anyone's idea of a good time.

Alec and Cheryl were in different boats, spinning circles, and careening into everyone around them. They hadn't seen me yet. I worked my way toward them, giving full throttle to the gutless boat engine.

By the time I reached the far side of the pool, Cheryl had been carried off in a current of boats. I floored my accelerator and hit Alec from behind, sending him spinning around and bouncing off the side wall. It got his attention.

"Jared!" he said, calling out over the noise all around us. "I thought they had you locked up in the ticket booth."

"I escaped."

He bumped me, and before I knew it we were moving in a circle around the outer edge of the pool, bumping each other.

"So, how do you like our school?" I asked him.

"You came to the bumper boats to ask me about school?" he said, sideswiping me.

I came around, pinning him against the dock. "I came to tell you something you might be too busy to notice."

"I notice everything." He tried to squeeze his way past, but I stayed just in front of him, keeping him pushed up against the dock.

"You might not notice *this*."

"Come on, Jared," he said. "I paid good money for this ride—those were my last tickets."

"I'll give you new tickets," I said to him. "Just listen."

I leaned forward, getting as close to him as I could, and said as quietly as I could under the circumstances. "You need to watch yourself," I told him. "Because there are some people who aren't too happy with your success. I just felt I should warn you."

Then his face hardened as he looked at me. "Are you threatening me?"

But before I could answer I was hit so hard from behind that my boat spun circles, and my head was slow to catch up. It was Cheryl.

"You were a sitting duck," she said. "It was my moral obligation to nail you."

The ride attendant called the boats in, and the kids that resisted got pulled back to the dock with a long hook. Alec hopped out of his boat, but my knobby knees were stuck. He came up to me, leaned over me, and said, not too loud, but loud enough for Cheryl to hear, "Don't think I don't know about you and those awful things you made Cheryl do in the Shadow Club."

"What's this all about?" asked Cheryl, but before I could explain myself, Alec put his arm around her and led her away.

"He's just a little jealous, that's all," he said. "He'll get over it."

I didn't even try to stammer out any further explanation, because I knew that no matter what I said or denied, I would look as guilty as a corporate executive in a news interview. So I just sat there with my legs uncomfortably wedged into the tiny boat until the carny came to shoo me out.

It began less than half an hour later.

There were several versions of the story, but when you put them all together you come up with this: Alec and Cheryl were sitting in the heated dance canopy, eating hot dogs and listening to a bad country western band. There were other kids at the tables around them, and a few people on the dance floor. Everyone was having a good old country time, until Alec started taking a few sips from his Dr Pepper. He complained that it tasted funny and very innocently took off the plastic lid, to reveal that the Dr Pepper shared the cup with a hair ball the size of King Kong. In fact, if you believe the various accounts, the cup had more hair than soda. In a few seconds Alec's face went through every shade of the visible spectrum before he leaped up, accidentally dumping the table and the hairy Dr Pepper right into Cheryl's lap.

Some say he puked right then and there, while others say he puked all over the dance floor. Still others claim he puked all over the lead singer's shiny red boots, but wherever his cookies landed, the fact that he tossed them was not in dispute. The story spread so quickly that a sonic boom echoed through the phone lines, and by morning the Furry Pepper Incident, as it was now being called, was quickly becoming a town legend like the Shadow Club itself . . . and that had me more scared than I had been in months.

I know what it's like to be trapped in a burning building—to have the smoke blind you, and the air turn into a furnace as you struggle to open a door—everything so far out of control that you can't even control your own bladder. I also know power. I've watched my will run unchecked, wreaking havoc among friends and enemies alike. I know how good it feels to be in control, and to feel that control reach beyond the limits of yourself until you feel larger than life. I know helplessness and I know power—and if I had my way, I would never want to be in either of those places again, because while one might burn your body, the other burns your soul.

If anything good came from the Shadow Club's dark adventure, it was the knowledge that I was capable of incredible acts of bravery, as well as profound acts of malice. Knowing the bad stuff is there is a good thing, I think, because you can always see it coming. You can protect yourself. You can chase it away before it takes hold and does any damage. But you can't fight what you can't see—and far too many kids didn't see the Furry Pepper Incident for what it really was . . . who didn't know that even the Great Flood began with a single drop of rain.

"Did you do it?"

Cheryl accosted me in a dead-end hallway in the math department. We were both late for class, but then, what choice did we have? Neither of us were willing to talk about this during passing time, when ears with the sensitivity of Geiger counters were hyperextended to hear gossip.

"Do you *think* I did it?" I asked.

"Are you going to play games with me?"

I shifted my heavy math book to my other hand.

"I suppose if I pleaded 'the fifth' you'd take my silence as guilt, wouldn't you? Why are you even asking if I've already been tried and convicted?"

"Did you do it?" she demanded again.

I found myself getting more and more angry that she, of all people, thought I was still capable of that.

"If I had a new girlfriend," I asked her, "would you put a clump of Bigfoot in her Coke?"

"No," she said, grimacing at the thought. "Of course not."

"Then how could you think that I would?"

She stood silently for a moment. I could see her shoulders relax. "So you're saying that you didn't do it."

I held out my book. "Do you want me to swear on my math book?"

"No," she said. The second bell rang, announcing that we were officially late without an excuse. "Alec says you threatened him."

"I *warned* him that there were some kids who aren't too happy with him. He just assumed I meant me."

"Are you . . . jealous of him, because he's going out with me?"

I wish I could have flatly denied it. I mean, what kind of moron admits to his former girlfriend's face that he's jealous? I guess I was that moron.

"Yeah," I told her. "Yeah, I am, a little . . . but that's *not* what this is about."

And then, to my amazement, she said something that no one had said to me for a long time.

"I believe you."

I should have shut my mouth then—quit while I was ahead—but of course I didn't.

"Actually, I kinda like Alec," I said. "I mean, he's an okay guy, once you get past his perfection problem."

She looked at me sideways, and that one look told me I was done for.

"Just what do you mean by that?"

"Well, just . . . um . . . that he's weird about being good at everything."

"There is nothing wrong with aiming high."

"There is when you're hunting ducks with a bazooka." By now I was so far into it there was no sense pulling back. "I mean, overkill must be the guy's middle name. It's like he would die if someone else got to be the center of attention."

She crossed her arms in her prosecutor posture.

"If he's so totally into himself," she said, far too calmly, "then why is he helping *me* run for class president?"

I stumbled over my own thoughts for a moment, wondering when she had decided to run, and why I didn't know about it. There was a time when I would have been first to know.

"That's great," I said. "I'm glad he'll be helping your campaign." And then I added, "Prove me wrong about him—and I'll eat my shoe."

"You're on," she said, shaking my hand. "Only I get to pick which one—I want to make sure it's nice and grungy."

She turned and strode off to class, but I couldn't let her go—not yet, because there was something I had to tell her—something I had been thinking about since the moment I heard about the hair ball.

"I've been thinking of reconvening the Shadow Club."

My words stopped her dead in her tracks, but she didn't turn around. She just stood there for a few seconds, her back still turned.

"I thought maybe we could all get together and stop things from happening to Alec," I told her.

"You won't need to stop it, because nothing else will happen," she said, and continued on to class.

The administrators of our school district haven't quite come to grips with the twenty-first century, or even the twentieth, for that matter. Our desks are the same shellacked, pen-carved relics they used fifty years ago. There are still holes for inkwells in the corner. We're not required to wear uniforms, but every Friday we still have to dress up for assembly. We also have that rare animal called a "junior high school"—seventh, eighth, and ninth grades all together, leaving only three grades for our senior high school. If it were up to our district superintendent I'm sure we would all be in little red schoolhouses that dotted the coastline.

I really didn't mind the junior high school thing. I mean, sure, I wanted to be in high school, but there was something to be said about never having a freshman year. Our town has only one junior high and one senior high—massive buildings across town from each other—built in the days when schools were giant institutions like prisons, which meant that few things would change when I made the move from ninth grade to tenth grade, other than the length of my run every morning. Same basic kids, same basic attitudes—and what you sowed in kindergarten, you were still reaping in twelfth grade.

Since the senior high had only one feeding school, it had been decided some years ago that during the winter lull after Christmas vacation and before the standardized tests, elections would be held for next year's class president. Whoever won the honor in ninth grade would walk right into senior high, master of tenth grade.

Nominations came during the next Friday's assembly. The assembly featured a former state representative who was so old we were afraid he would expire before his parking meter outside. Following him were our official presidential nominations. It was common knowledge by now that Cheryl planned to run. She had weathered the storm of the Shadow Club far better than I had. Rather than earning her the label of "questionable kid," as it did for me, her involvement left an aura of awe around her. It was just the kind of quality that could get a person elected, and she knew it. Of course you couldn't nominate yourself, and so when the call came for nominations I quickly raised my hand to nominate her. Turns out I didn't need to. Alec held his hand high right next to her. He drew the principal's attention as he always drew everyone's attention. He was called on first.

"I nominate Cheryl Gannett," he said.

"I second that," shouted someone else.

"I accept," said Cheryl as if there would be any doubt.

I observed as the nominations went around the auditorium. In all there were about a dozen, but when push came to shove, few of them were seconded, and so those kids names never made the list. In the end it was Cheryl, Tommy Nickols, who was expected to be the school's valedictorian, and Katrina Mendelson, who had been trying to get elected since fourth grade. As the principal called for final nominations, one more hand went up. The hand belonged to Calvin Horner—a snively kid with a bit of a speech impediment and teeth almost as yellow as his hair. I wondered what on earth would possess him to stand up and speak in front of a crowd when it was always such a chore for him to answer a simple question in class.

"I would like to nominate Alec Smartz for class president," Calvin said.

There were more seconds than I could count, followed by a low afterburn of grumbles from those who were not pleased. I turned to see Alec shrug innocently at a gaping Cheryl as he said loudly, "I guess I accept."

That's when I saw Calvin Horner give a little nod to Alec, making it very clear that this was not a spontaneous act.

On Monday I came to school with a shoe box under my arm and approached Cheryl at her locker. Holding it like a waiter with a tray, I pulled off the lid.

"Canvas or leather," I said. "Your choice."

Inside, of course, were one of my dress shoes and a sneaker so grungy it could be considered hazardous waste.

"Oh, shut up."

I had to admit I felt bad for her, and guilty for having rubbed her nose in it. I shoved the shoe box under my arm.

"Sorry," I said. "I mean . . . I'm sorry Alec wasn't really behind you. It would have been great if you could have worked together."

"Actually," said Cheryl, "things will still work out. Chances are that one of us will win, and the other will take second place, which means we'd be each other's vice president."

"I don't think so," I said. "Two possibilities—assuming Katrina or Tommy don't pull it out—either (A) he'll win and you'll be his vice president; or (B) you'll win, and he will melt like the Wicked Witch of the West."

"Well, now you're just being nasty."

"No, I'm serious. Alec is not a vice presidential kind of guy. He might say so now, but that's just because he doesn't believe it will ever happen."

She slammed her locker, incredibly angry about how sure I was, and maybe a bit bothered by the knowledge that I was right. "That's your opinion," she said, "and if I didn't want your vote, I would tell you exactly where you could put that opinion."

There was a commotion farther down the hall. I didn't take much note of it until we both heard the name Alec

Smartz mumbled more than once. We went over to find out what was going on.

"Did you hear what happened to Alec?" said a kid who was anxious to tell anyone who would listen.

"What?" asked Cheryl apprehensively.

"He got skunked," the kid said. "Him and his whole family."

Cheryl's first reaction was relief that it hadn't been anything really bad, but that relief was quickly overshadowed by suspicion. "Wait a second . . . skunks aren't out this time of year—"

"Maybe he went poking in a hole where it was hibernating, or something," I suggested.

"Nope," said the kid, "it happened in their van. They got in it this morning, the skunk popped out from under a seat, and the rest is history."

Suddenly I got that same sense of looming doom I felt when I first heard about the hair ball in his soda. Unless skunks had acquired the ability to teleport, it was clear that it had been intentionally slipped into the Smartzes' family van.

Alec didn't show up for school that day, but he was there the next day. Although he tried to act as if nothing was wrong, that burned-rubbery smell of skunk surrounded him like killer BO, no matter how many demusking baths he took. And as for that minivan, it couldn't have been more totaled if it had fallen off a cliff.

Although Alec didn't accuse me to my face, the accusation was there all the same. It was in the way he looked at me—or refused to look at me. The second day after the skunking he came up to me as we were leaving English class, one of the few classes we had together. He didn't just bump into me—he made a point of coming up to me, and, although he hadn't said a word to me in two days, he looked at me, grinning in a way that I couldn't quite read, and said, "Nice shirt."

I figured he was just trying to bother me, you know, the way you say "nice socks" to someone whose socks are perfectly fine, making him wonder for the rest of the day what the heck is wrong with his socks. I just stored it away in my brain.

The weird thing Alec said wasn't the only thing bothering me. In fact, he didn't bother me as much as the looks I got from other kids—suspicious glances that were more obvious than ever before.

As I pulled books from my locker the next day, someone behind me said, "Good one, Jared!"

I spun on my heel, but when I looked at the kids around me, I couldn't tell who it had been. It could have been any of them. All of them. A hallway full of faces convinced that the Shadow Club and I had been responsible for the skunk as well as the hair ball.

That afternoon I slipped messages into six different lockers—messages that called the Shadow Club back from the dead.

The Ghosties

S OME PLACES, LIKE some people, age well, and others don't. They fall into disrepair and disrespect. That's how it was with the old marina. The old marina was on the north end of town, about a mile past the lighthouse ruin. The place wasn't exactly a picture postcard. The water was slick with a perpetual oily scum, and speckled with bits of trash. The wooden piles that held up the fishing pier had been eaten away, making the pier a use-at-your-own-risk kind of place. Of course, there were still die-hard fishermen—old-timers mostly—who set out from the marina every morning before dawn, but otherwise the place was a desolate relic of another time.

At the far bank of the inlet sat the half-submerged skeleton of a ferry that had been washed up during a storm, ten years back. On the south side of the inlet was a seawall made of eroding concrete, dripping rust from the reinforcing iron bars that now lay exposed to the sea. Just above that seawall, overlooking the marina, was the Ghosties.

The Ghosties was a graveyard of sorts—a boatyard of the

damned. Fishing boats, sailboats, cabin cruisers, you name it, they eventually found their way up to the Ghosties. Of course, few people would admit that when they towed their boat there, they were bringing their vessel to its eternal rest. The boats were brought here for repairs, or for storage. They sat in rusted trailers with flat tires, or cradled in scaffolding, waiting for their owners to return. But those owners would die of old age, or move on to other hobbies, leaving the forlorn boats to haunt the Ghosties, tortured by a beautiful view of the ocean that they would never set keel in again.

The sight of the old boats had always impressed me. They looked so much larger on dry land than in the sea—vessels that seemed so natural when bobbing with the tide, and so awkward and alien when dragged up on dry land.

The Ghosties had always been a great place for hide-and-seek when I was younger. Kids used to play it all the time here, until some kid fell off the seawall and drowned. After that the Ghosties had been fenced off . . . but when you live near the ocean, it doesn't take long for the salt air to rust through a chain-link fence.

"So what do you think?" Tyson asked as we meandered through the maze of abandoned boats.

"It'll do," I told him.

It had been his idea to meet here rather than at the Shadow Club's old meeting place—that old foundation in the woods we had called "Stonehenge." Too many bad memories there—and besides, if people were starting to suspect us, that would be the first place they'd look. This secret meeting required a new secret place.

"This way," said Tyson, leading me between the peeling hulls, until we came to the remains of a tugboat left to rot within a steel cradle barely large enough to hold it. It was clearly the largest boat in the Ghosties, and it sat there like a monument, just by the edge of the seawall, overlooking the ocean.

A swell smashed against the seawall some ten feet below, sending salt spray across the old boat's hull. "Someone bought it for salvage, I think," Tyson said. "They gutted it and left its shell up here."

On its lower hull was a hole about two feet wide. No doubt this tug had an interesting story to tell, but I suspected it never would.

"I used to come here when things got real bad," Tyson said, poking his head up through the hole in the hull. "Great place to go when you don't want to be found. Have a look."

I leaned into the hole in the hull. The space smelled of mildew and diesel fuel, but I couldn't see a thing.

Then I heard the far-off rattle of the rusty fence, which meant either our meeting was about to begin, or we were being chased away. I hurried off toward the sound, but found myself lost in the maze of boats. It was Jason Perez who found me, rather than the other way around.

"Hey," he said. I turned around to see him keeping his distance. "So, like, where are the others?"

"You're the first."

"Oh." He didn't seem to like the idea of being first. "I hope you know, I ditched band practice for this." He took a few steps closer, and so did I, hoping the discomfort between us would fade with each step. It didn't. "Are you sure the others are coming?"

"No."

"Well, if they don't show," he said, "I'm bailing. I don't even know why I came in the first place."

"I'm glad you did." I reached out my hand to him, and he looked at it for a long moment. Finally he accepted it, shaking halfheartedly, but then he tensed as he saw someone over my shoulder. I turned to see Tyson coming up behind us.

"It's okay," I told Jason. "I invited him."

"Oh . . . uh . . . nice to see you, Tyson."

"Yeah, yeah." said Tyson. I guess you couldn't expect any more from the two of them. I mean, the last time they were this close to each other, Jason and the others were trying to drown him with their bare hands.

"So . . . like, you're a member of the club now, Tyson?" Jason asked.

"No . . . I'm kind of an independent observer."

"There is no club!" said a voice behind us. We turned to see Darren Collins coming out from behind a broken catamaran. "The Shadow Club doesn't exist, and I'm guessing we're here to make sure of it."

"You guessed right," I told him. I have to admit I was surprised he had come at all. Of all the members of the club, he was the one who had pulled the farthest away from the rest of us. He wouldn't talk to us, wouldn't acknowledge us in class. It wasn't so much a cold shoulder, as a "no shoulder." It was as if the only way he could get past it was simply to cut the Shadow Club out of his life. He played basketball the same way—blocking out everything but his teammates, the ball, and the basket. That's what made him so good.

Abbie showed up next, looking as beautiful as ever, dressed one week ahead of the fashions. "OK," she said, "I'm dying to find out what possible reason you have for getting us all together."

Karin "O. P." Han showed up with Randall. She didn't say much, but as with the others, her eyes darted to Tyson, and looked away, ashamed.

"My sister chickened out," Randall said. "Cheryl's not coming."

"Big surprise," said Darren.

"Too bad," I said, trying to hide how disappointed I really felt. "But we can do this without her."

"Do what?" asked Abbie.

"Duh," said Randall, his same old obnoxious self, "figure out which one of us is pranking on Alec Smartz."

Everyone glanced at one another with the same suspicion that the other kids in school heaped on us.

"What makes you so sure it was one of us?" I asked him.

He looked at the others, one by one, and then his thoughts seemed to turn in on himself. "I don't know," he said. "I just figured . . ."

And that was half the problem right there. If even the members of the Shadow Club believed it was one of our own, how would we ever gain one another's trust again?

Tyson and I led them up to the old tugboat and through the hole in the hull. When our eyes had adjusted to the light spilling in from the hole below, and the dozens of little separations in the old boat's wooden planks, we found ourselves in a strange and very private world. The empty shell of the tugboat's keel was like an upside-down attic. Although the space was about thirty feet long, and seven feet high, it still felt claustrophobic. I didn't like it. Rats hide in forgotten places like this, I thought. And I'm not a rat. The fact that we had to hide at all made me regret having even called them together. I mean, was Alec Smartz really worth all this trouble? And if my heart really *was* in the right place, then why was my spirit confined to the moldering shell of an abandoned boat?

"We didn't do anything to Alec Smartz," I said, once everyone was up inside our new meeting place. I didn't ask them, I told them. If there was one thing in this world that

I knew, it was that all of us—even Randall—had come through the ordeal better than when we started. None of us would pull that sort of mean-spirited prank on anyone ever again. Although it was dim in the shell of the old boat, I could see enough of their faces to know I was right.

"So, like, we're supposed to prove our innocence before the whole world blames us, right?" said Jason.

"It's not about proving our innocence," I told him. "It's about stopping the pranks."

"How are we supposed to stop the pranks if we don't know who's pulling them?" asked Darren.

"We do some detective work," I said. "We find out."

"Why should we care a rat's butt about Alec Smartz, anyway?" asked Randall.

"Because we started it. None of this would be happening if we didn't start the pranks last fall."

"Statistics show," said O. P., "that the most notorious of criminals often have copycats—and sometimes those copycats are worse than the ones they're copying."

"Oh, come on," said Abbie, tossing back her hair, "we're not exactly serial killers."

"No," said Tyson, "but you came pretty close to killing me."

Tyson had been so quiet, sitting all the way up toward the bow, that we had almost forgotten he was there. It sobered us up a little bit.

"We set the pattern," I told them. "We were the ones who put the idea in people's heads, and now they're picking up where we left off. I don't know who it is, but I do know that the pranks are going to get worse and worse, just like they did the first time. When we formed the Shadow Club, it's like we let something loose in this town that didn't die when we burned the charter."

"You mean like a demon or something?" asked Randall.

"Now you're getting me all spooked," said Jason with a nervous chuckle.

"Call it what you want," I told them. "A demon—or just a bad idea—but either way it's not going away until we find a way to shoot it with a silver bullet."

"I thought that was for a werewolf," said Jason.

"Get a clue," said Abbie.

I let the thought sit with them for a few long moments. The wind blew across the hole in the hull, like someone breathing across the mouth of a bottle, and the whole tugboat began to resonate with a faint deep moan.

That's when Darren said, "I'm outta here." He stood up, balancing himself on the slanted floor beneath him. "I've got better things to do than start dreaming up problems that don't exist."

I was too stunned to say a thing.

Abbie stood up next. "I mean, really, Jared, you've got yourself all worked up into a panic for no reason."

"What a waste of an afternoon," said Randall.

"Wait a second," I said, just beginning to see how totally I had misread them. "Don't you care at all about what's happening?"

Jason shrugged. "People were pulling pranks long before the Shadow Club existed," he said. "Just because they're doing it now doesn't mean we, like, *inspired* them or something. It probably has nothing to do with us."

"Yeah," agreed Abbie. "Alec Smartz has made as many enemies as he has made friends."

I looked to O. P., who had seemed to be more on my side than any of the others, but now she looked away. "I think maybe you're being too paranoid, Jared."

I stood there watching them leave, not sure what to say that could convince them they were wrong. That, yeah, maybe I was paranoid, but sometimes that cleared your vision more than it clouded it.

"The Shadow Club's dead," said Darren. "Let it stay that way." Then he slipped out through the hull, leaving Tyson and me alone. Tyson didn't move from his little perch way up at the bow. He must have sat in that spot when he used to come here by himself.

"That went well," he said.

"Oh, shut up."

I thought the meeting was over, but when Tyson and I slipped out through the hole, we were met by an unexpected guest.

"I could have told you they wouldn't go for it," said

Cheryl. I turned to see her standing just a few yards away. I wondered whether she had been there all along, listening, or if she had just arrived in time to see everyone else desert.

"Easy for you to say, now that they've all gone." I was a bit angry that she hadn't done anything to help, but also grateful that she decided to come after all.

"They've got nothing to gain by helping you find the new prankster. The further away from it they stay, the better for them."

"That's what they think, but they're wrong. It's going to come back in their faces, the way it's come back in mine."

A wave broke on the seawall below us and sent up a burst of foam that soaked Tyson.

"Oh, man . . ." Tyson used it as an excuse to leave, but I knew he felt uncomfortable being there—a kind of third wheel between Cheryl and me. When Tyson was gone, she took a step closer.

"Alec thinks there ought to be a new club—one that will cancel out the Shadow Club."

"One that *he's* in charge of?"

"It could be a good thing. All right, I'll admit he's a little bit conceited, but his heart's in the right place."

Hearing that made me suddenly feel the chill of the ocean breeze.

"Does he know how much you stand up for him?"

"No," answered Cheryl, "but he knows how much I stand up for *you*."

That shut me up real quick. On the one hand it felt good to know that she would still stick up for me. On the other hand, Cheryl always knew the exact words to say to win a conversation with me. Lately reading her had been like looking into a one-way mirror. I could only tell what was behind her words in a certain rare light, which wasn't shining today.

I couldn't look her in the eye, so I turned and stepped over to the ledge, where the seawall rose from below and met the flat mesa of the Ghosties. It was an unguarded precipice, and I marveled at how stupid we all were to play here when we were little. I longed for that kind of stupidity again, when I didn't know enough to see danger around me. Far off I heard the fence rattle as Tyson made his way out of the Ghosties. The sound brought me back to the here and now.

"Maybe we'd better go," I told Cheryl.

Another wave sprayed up over the ledge, dousing us, as if the sea itself was trying to chase us away. I heard the fence rattle again, and figured it must have just been the wind. We turned away from the tugboat, and left together, but it was painfully obvious to both of us that we were very much apart.

The next afternoon, I went with Tyson down to the community pool. One of my many New Year's resolutions had been to teach Tyson to swim. I figured it was one small way to try and make up for the part I played in almost drowning him last fall.

At first I took him to the pool several times a week, but, like all New Year's resolutions, my resolve faded pretty quickly. I hadn't given him a lesson for more than three weeks. But now, with so many things squirming around in my brain, I welcomed the chance to focus my thoughts on something else. I dragged Tyson down to the pool, with him resisting all the way.

"It's cold." "I'm tired." "I got too much homework." "I think I got an earache."

Tyson was never an eager learner when it came to anything, but today I wasn't taking no for an answer.

Our local pool had a personality all its own. First of all it wasn't even called a pool, it was called a "natatorium," which I guess was a gymnasium for swimming. With a fancy name like that, they could charge two bucks to get in. The natatorium had an Olympic-sized pool, and huge windows that were always so fogged it defeated the purpose of having windows in the first place. As for the pool itself, well, it was about as clouded as the windows. I used to wear goggles when I swam, but stopped because I got tired of looking at all those unidentifiable bits of floating organic matter. There are just some things I'd rather not know about.

Tyson had managed to master the dog paddle pretty early on in our lessons, and now he proudly huffed and puffed his way through six laps like a Labrador, while I swam a fairly lame, but effective crawl.

"Listen, do you want to learn to swim or not?" I snapped as he tried to climb out of the pool.

"What do you call what I just did? That was six laps!"

I pulled him back into the water. "Six dog laps," I corrected. "That's not even one human lap, Fido."

In the lane beside us, which was reserved for the more serious swimmers, someone did a quick flip turn and splashed super-chlorinated water up my nose.

"Ughh!" I sneezed and tried to clear my burning sinuses.

"Serves you right," Tyson said.

When I looked up to see who had splashed me, I caught sight of Drew Landers, our school's number one swimmer, peering out at me from beneath his armpit for an instant, as he stroked forward, toward the deep end of the pool.

"He did that on purpose!" I said.

"What, is like everyone out to get you now?" Tyson said. "You're starting to sound like me. That's scary."

"Tell me about it."

Drew Landers, however, did have a reason to hold a grudge against me—after all, the Shadow Club had pranked him exceptionally well during that first round of pranks, when it all still felt like fun, before it started getting dangerous. We had paid Drew a midnight visit, and peeled back the grungy socks from his feet as he slept. Then we painted his toenails red and put the socks back on. He didn't take them off again until swim practice the next day, and, let me tell you, it made quite an impression on the swim team—not to mention the coach, who scheduled him an immediate visit to Mr. Greene for tender guidance. I had to admit, though, Drew did manage to turn the whole situation around. Rather than clean off his toes, he painted every other toenail white, so his feet proudly displayed our school colors of red and white. He said it was a sign of school spirit. Since he was the team captain, and one of the cool-defining personalities of our school, the entire swim team followed his lead and went the rest of the season with red-and-white-painted toenails. I think this is how really stupid traditions are born.

"C'mon," I told Tyson, trying to forget about Drew. "I'll teach you the crawl."

"Tyson McGaw never crawls."

"Then Tyson McGaw drowns."

"Have you ever known a dog that drowned?"

He had a point, but he wasn't getting out of it so fast. "Would you like it better if I called it 'freestyle'?"

"Yeah. I could get into freestyle."

I tried to work with him on the rhythm of his breathing, but then took another blast of water in the face. It gagged me, and I coughed up like half a lung. When my eyes cleared, I saw Drew Landers standing in the pool beside us, doing some sort of swimmer's stretch with his arm behind his head like a contortionist.

"Your stroke bites the biscuit," Drew told me. "If Tyson wants swimming lessons, he should have asked me."

"Yeah, right," said Tyson. "Like you'd care."

Drew only shrugged. "It's a community service," he said. "Community service always looks good on your permanent record."

"Thanks, but we're doing fine by ourselves," I told him, and tried to get back to the lesson. I hoped Drew would just push off and continue his laps, but he didn't.

"I hear you've been pranking on Alec Smartz."

I took a deep, slow breath, and tried not to let anger seep into my voice. "You heard wrong."

"That skunk was rank and righteous!" Drew said. "Was that the first time you ever skunked someone?"

"No!" I insisted. "I mean yes! I mean neither! I didn't do it!"

"Hey, you know what they say: *He who denied it, supplied it.*"

"No," said Tyson, "that's for farts."

Drew shrugged. "Skunks, farts, not much of a difference, is there?" Drew reached up and did his contortionist stretch again. "Can't say Alec didn't deserve it, though—the way he's been strutting around like he's God's gift to whatever."

"If you hate him so much," I said, "then how do we know that *you* didn't do it?"

Drew slipped his goggles back on. "Because I lack the psycho-factor—but not you. In fact, put the two of you together and there's enough psycho to make national head-lines."

I was going to say something back—something truly wise and profound, or at least just flip him off, but before I could, he slipped back under the water and pushed off, swimming away as silently as a shark.

"That really ticks me off," I grumbled.

Tyson nodded. "Wanna go on a rampage?"

I shivered, feeling cold with half of my body out of the water. "That's not even funny."

The Microscope and the Magnifying Glass

I HAD TO accept that, in the real world, there was no such thing as being innocent until proven guilty. Everyone was happy to assume I was guilty, and I was the only one who could prove my innocence. That would take some serious investigation.

I'm not much of a detective. I used to read all those three-minute mystery books, but I never had the patience to figure them out, so I'd just turn to the back to find the answer. I always seemed to miss the details that were most important. While Tyson wasn't stupid, he was no great brain either, and so together the two of us felt less like Holmes and Watson, and more like Beavis and Butthead.

The hair ball trail was cold. There was no sense even trying to solve that one. So Tyson and I spent the next afternoon on a skunk-out. Cheryl had been right when she said that skunks weren't out this time of year, and even if they were, it would have taken quite a lot of effort to catch one. Seemed to me that the skunk had to come from the Nature

Center. It was a small building down a dirt road, famous for grammar school field trips, and an adopt-a-snake program that hadn't gone over very well. Tyson and I saw what we expected when we went in: metal cages filled with everything from guinea pigs to porcupines, and glass aquariums that housed iguanas and many an unadopted python. The ranger, or whoever it was who ran the place, wasn't there, but we did find one of our classmates, Jodi Lattimer, cleaning out a rabbit cage.

The half grin on Tyson's face as we approached testified to the crush he had on Jodi. She was one of those down-to-earth girls who never seemed to have a problem with being elbow deep in compost. She was pretty but found a variety of ways to hide it. Today it was a denim baseball cap turned backward to cover her long blond hair. She was the kind of girl I might have had a crush on if I hadn't known Tyson was already there.

"Hi, guys. What's up?" she said. I stepped forward, trying to figure the best way to say this without sounding too terribly stupid. "We were wondering if you, by any chance, had misplaced a skunk."

She grinned, knowing exactly why we were asking, and Tyson grinned back, probably thinking her smile was for him. "You mean had a skunk been *stolen*, don't you?" she said.

"Naah," said Tyson. "Can't steal a wild animal, they belong to everyone." I rolled my eyes.

"Well," said Jodi, "apparently somebody thought this

skunk belonged to them." She went on to tell us that somebody had pried open a back window and had run off with it
a few nights ago. "God knows how they got it out of here
without it spraying all over them—unless, of course, they
drugged it."

We went around the side of the building to the window
that had been pried open, searching for footprints or something, but the ground was hard, dry, and covered with dense
pine needles. Nothing to give away who it might have been.

"We don't have much to go on," commented Tyson.

Jodi crossed her arms and smirked, "Come on, you guys,
the way you're talking you'd think you were investigating a
murder."

"Maybe we are," I said. "After all, the skunk hasn't been
seen since it escaped from Alec's van."

She laughed at that, and then I noticed Tyson starting to
get all fidgety, annoyed that I had made her laugh instead of
him.

"If you want to do a real investigation, you ought to talk
to my father," she said.

"Oh yeah!" said Tyson. "He interrogated me once." And
then his face went slightly purple from that particular foot in
his mouth. Jodi's father was a high-ranking police deputy,
which was a pretty dull job in this town. Usually.

"Didn't he talk to the Smartzes already?"

"Probably, but I'm sure he'd like to know of your interest
in the case."

As I was still the prime suspect, talking to the police was not currently high on my list of fun activities. At least not until I had my own suspects. "Let's just leave this a private investigation," I told her.

"Yeah," said Tyson, grinning dumbly at her. "Kind of like 'intimate.'"

I went through a list of interrogation questions I had scrawled on my note pad: Were there any suspicious characters in the area? Have animals been stolen before? Blah blah blah. Every question was answered with a simple "No." When there were no questions left we said our good-byes, but before we headed back down the dirt road, I couldn't stop myself from turning to her and saying, "You know that I didn't do it, don't you?"

Jodi just shrugged. "Whatever you say." She adjusted her cap and went inside to finish tending to the rabbits.

"I think she likes me," said Tyson as we walked off.

I was about to say "Dream on," but stopped myself. Instead I said, "Maybe so." Because in all truth I couldn't tell what anyone was thinking anymore.

On Monday the school was plastered, and I mean *plastered* with campaign banners, spread like wallpaper so you couldn't see the color of the walls. **Vote for Tommy Nickols**, some of them said, **The thinking man's candidate** (which obviously wasn't true, because by choosing "thinking man's" rather than "thinking person's" he had thoughtlessly alienated the entire female vote). **Vote for Katrina Mendelson**, other banners proclaimed. **Isn't it time?** Cheryl had her share as well. Hers had no clever slogan but a practical and attractive list of the changes she planned to make. She included things like economic sanctions against old man Solerno until he changed the recipe of his god-awful pizza, and raising the temperature of the gym from subarctic conditions.

But by far the most banners, posters, fliers, and signs were for candidate Alec Emery Smartz Jr. I couldn't help but overhear a conversation between Alec and Cheryl near her locker.

"What did you do," she said, "hire elves to paint them for you?"

Alec laughed it off. "In a way," he said. "A lot of the seventh and eighth graders just volunteered."

"You know, that really shouldn't be allowed," said Cheryl. "I mean, they can't even vote in the ninth-grade election."

Alec sighed. "If it bothers you that much, I'll take them down."

But Cheryl, of course, backed off. "No, no," she said. "Anyway, it's quality not quantity, and after all, my banners say more than just my name." She smiled at him, he smiled back, and they toddled off to class together as if there were no tension between them. But I knew Cheryl better than that, and I was beginning to wonder which was more important to her now, their budding romance or the competition between them.

"I'm glad Alec has so much support," Cheryl told me the next day in science lab. "Especially being so new to town. He's made lots of friends very quickly."

"And lots of enemies."

She shrugged it off, but it clearly bothered her. "Kids that don't like him just don't know him." Then she quickly changed the subject. "Any more luck with the Shadow Club?" I put my eye to the microscope, where I caught several paramecia wandering around between the thin sheets of glass. "No," I answered. "I'm running my own investigation without them."

"Really," said Cheryl. "So is Alec. He still thinks you pulled the pranks and says he wants to prove to me what a sniveling waste of life you are. I told him I already knew that—but it doesn't mean you pulled those pranks." She gave me a smile that made her most biting comments go down smoothly. "Anyway," she said, "you don't have to worry, because I don't believe it was you."

"So convince him."

"I can't. Anytime we talk about you, we always start yelling at each other, so Alec and I have a rule that we are not allowed to discuss you anymore."

"Does that come before or after the rule that you're not allowed to be better than him in anything?"

Cheryl turned the microscope focus until the lens cracked the fragile glass slide.

"Oh, great." She reached to prepare another slide.

As I looked up I saw several kids around the lab quickly avert their eyes. They had been watching us, listening to us, and I got that feeling again. O. P. said it was just paranoia, but I don't know. One girl rolled her neck, as if she hadn't been looking at all. Another kid adjusted his baseball cap when I looked at him, as if he hadn't been motioning to his lab partner to look our way. Suddenly I began to feel like those paramecia beneath the microscope's eye, unable to squirm out of view.

I was late leaving school that day, and there weren't many people left in the halls. Usually those halls are so noisy, you can't hear your own thoughts, but with most of the school gone, even the slightest noises sounded as if they were blasted over the loudspeaker. The sound of tearing paper echoed down the locker-lined hallway, and I followed it to the first floor, where I found Austin Pace tearing down one of Cheryl's big campaign banners.

"What are you doing?"

He turned to me, then went back to his task. "Isn't it obvious?" He crumpled the banner down, so it would fit in a trash can. It wasn't like he was doing this in secret—I mean, there were still some kids and teachers wandering the halls, but he didn't care. It was as if he wanted to be caught. He was daring people to make him stop.

"What's the point?"

"The point is, after what you and Cheryl did, she doesn't deserve to run for class president, or anything else. You might have been the mastermind, but *she* was the one who broke my ankle." By now he had crumpled the banner down to the size of a basketball. He tossed it toward the Hefty-lined trash can. It dropped in without even touching the rim. "Three pointer," he said. "Nothing but bag."

He crossed the hallway, to tear down another of Cheryl's banners. I grabbed his wrist to stop him, but he shook me off. Then he shoved me. I shoved him back, and we both stood there, waiting to see if it would escalate. Instead of going for me again, he reached over and tore down the banner.

"Y'know, my mom invited Cheryl over for dinner, too," Austin said. "She was smarter than you, though. She refused." He wadded up the banner. "Hey, why don't you help me? You once asked what would make me happy, and right now you helping me tear down *her* banners would warm the bottom of my heart."

He waited, but I didn't move.

"No, I didn't think so. I'm sure you'll even tell her that it was me who tore them down. Well, good. I want you to tell her."

But I had already decided not to tell Cheryl about it. Resentment had more faces and more sideways glances than a deck of cards, and if this was how Austin wanted to play out his hand, I wasn't going to stop him, and I wasn't going to give him the satisfaction of tattling to Cheryl. Part of me even agreed with Austin. After what the Shadow Club had done, Cheryl should have stayed out of the election the way I resigned from the track team—but that was her decision to make, and I wasn't going to judge her for it. My judging days were over.

"Have fun with your anti-campaign," I told him, and left him alone to score whatever trash can baskets he felt he needed.

Austin's banner vandalism was just more evidence that the anger in our school was breeding like bacteria. I might not have been responsible for everyone's anger, but I had certainly been a carrier. I could only hope it wasn't about to become an epidemic.

By now the entire school was anxiously anticipating what would happen to Alec next. I knew that I was, and I was not looking forward to getting the blame, or the credit, as some kids at school would put it.

It happened after gym class—another class that Alec and I had together. We'd been doing tumbles and unimpressive moves on the parallel bars. I never minded gym, but I could tell Alec hated it. As he liked to enter any activity at the very top, he despised being forced to engage in sports in which he wasn't already the best—and though he claimed to be a whiz at any sport that involved a ball, he was an absolute klutz when it came to gymnastics. So when class was over and we hit the locker rooms, he wasn't in the best of moods. My gym locker was just a few feet away from his. Usually we faced in opposite directions when we dressed so we wouldn't have to deal with each other, but today he felt like striking up a conversation.

"You really must like that shirt," he said to me with a smirk on his face. "You wear it an awful lot."

It was the same shirt he had commented about once before. It was just a plain, old blue-buttoned shirt.

"So," I said. "It's comfortable."

"You should wash it once in a while," he suggested. "You might find it smells better."

"At least it doesn't smell like skunk," I said under my breath but loud enough for him to hear.

"You've got Cheryl fooled, but you haven't fooled me," he said. "And you'll get what you deserve sooner than you think."

I closed my locker. "Was that a threat?"

"Nope," he said, "because I won't sink down to your level."

He pulled out a hairbrush and a bottle of styling gel, then pumped some of the clear gel into his hand.

"You believe what you want," I told him, "but when the truth comes out, I'll be expecting a major apology from you."

He laughed at that, rubbing the gel between his hands, then brushing his hands through his perfect hair. Right about then I began to smell a chemical odor, like paint or varnish. Schools were filled with weird smells, so I didn't think about it at first, until I noticed the look on Alec's face. His hands were still moving through his hair, spreading the gel, but his hands weren't moving as freely as they should have been.

By now some other kids had begun to take notice.

"What the . . . what is this?"

His hands were still firmly pressed against the sides of his head. He tried to pull them away, but they weren't coming.

"This isn't my hair gel!"

As the smell around me grew stronger, I recognized it. My father and I had smelled it out in the garage when trying to glue back together some broken lawn furniture. It was the smell of Lunar Glue—a super-epoxy *"so strong it could hold the moon in orbit,"* went the slogan—and right now it was spread across Alec Smartz's entire head. Lunar Glue was a prank as old as time, and although it was always funny in TV and in movies, the reality wasn't so funny. It was like watching a hummingbird caught on flypaper.

I found myself backing away, as if putting distance between me and the sabotaged bottle of gel would cast the guilt off of my shoulders.

"Don't look at *me*," I said, but that's exactly where Alec was looking.

"What did you do to me!" he shouted, beginning to go red in the face. He tried to pull his hands away from his hair, but his head just tilted with the motion of his hands, bonded there, like a pot. Shirtless and barefoot he stumbled out of the locker room with me and a dozen other kids behind him. The bell had rung and the hall was filled with kids. Someone bumped his elbow. "Ahh," he screamed, and he spun like a turnstile.

"You're going down for this, Mercer," he said. "You're going down in a major way."

Through the crowd I saw Cheryl, wondering what on earth was going on.

"Alec?"

By now the group of kids around us had expanded, and more people took notice of Alec's strange shirtless position. Now Alec was the center of attention—the place he always wanted to be, but not quite the way that he wanted it.

"Alec, what's wrong?" asked Cheryl, looking to him, to me, then back to him again.

"I've been Lunar Glued," he said with a whine in his voice.

And that's when someone laughed. I don't know who it was, but that laugh started it. It was just a snicker at first, and then another, and then another.

"Shut up!" said Alec. "It's not funny!"

And he was right. It wasn't, and yet I found a grin coming to my face as well. It had to do with the way that he was just standing there, his hands in a permanent pose on the sides of his head, like a fashion model. A hummingbird on flypaper, horrible and helpless—but the mob's laughter was contagious. I found myself beginning to giggle, just one among the rising chorus of laughter, as Cheryl reached up and tried to pull his hands away from his head.

"Oh, Alec," she said, and she, too, started laughing.

It became uncontrollable. As awful and as terrible as it was—as cruel as it was—a part of all of us just had to laugh and laugh and laugh, until tears came to our eyes. But it wasn't everyone's laughter that Alec heard. It was mine and Cheryl's.

I Am Not Now
Nor Have I Ever Been
a Waste of Life

SOMETIMES I HAVE to close my eyes and put myself back in the burning lighthouse. It's kind of like scratching at a scab; it itches, and you know that's because it's healing, but you can't stop scratching it. Pretty soon it begins to bleed, and you've got to start healing all over again. They put these cones around dogs' heads to keep them from scratching wounds. I wish someone could put some kind of cone around me, because on the day Alec's hand got glued to his head, I couldn't help but scratch. I went down to the beach where Tyson and I had washed ashore, that day back in October. There were still plenty of reminders—like the burned timbers half buried in the sand. The smell of charred wood had mingled with the salty aroma of decaying kelp. The sound of the sea was a constant reminder, too—the rumble of the breakers and the hiss of the spray—such a comfort to some people, so threatening to me.

I walked the beach all that afternoon, looking at the

burned driftwood, listening to the uneasy echoes of the world around me in seashells, picking the scab.

I was so lost in my own thoughts, I didn't notice that I wasn't alone on the beach, until I practically walked into two kids heading the other way.

"Oh, sorry," I said. It took me a moment to register who they were. It was none other than Brett Whatley and our resident large dude, Moose SanGiorgio. After my fight with Brett the other week, he was the last person I wanted to see. As for Moose, well, he was kind of like human flavor enhancer; he wasn't much by himself, but somehow his linebacker presence doubled the intensity of whomever he was with. In this case it turned Brett Whatley from a general nuisance into a four-star general nuisance.

"We got a message for you from Alec Smartz," Brett said, then he tried to deliver a punch to my gut. He must have seen too many action movies, however, because he sort of did it in slow motion. I caught his fist in my open palm and squeezed, cracking all of his knuckles. It sounded like a bag of microwave popcorn.

"Arrggg!"

He pulled back his hand, grimacing, and almost fell to his knees.

"That's gotta hurt," said Moose.

Moose was actually a pretty intelligent guy when he was around intelligent people, but today he was taking his lead from a guy with the mental capacity of a canned ham. Still, I tried to address Moose's more sensible side.

"So, Moose, what's the deal here? Did Alec really send you guys to beat me up?"

"He hired us as bodyguards," Moose said happily. "The beating-you-up part was Brett's idea."

Brett grunted, still shaking his aching hand.

"What's Alec paying you?" I asked Moose.

"He says he'll give us positions in his cabinet when he gets elected class president."

"Get cash," I told him.

"I'll consider it."

Brett, having recovered, glared at me. "We're here to tell you that you'd better lay off Alec, or we may have to take steps."

"Ooh—that's a tough one," I said, and did a quick search through my long-term movie memory. "Ah! I've got it! Michael Beihn said that in *The Abyss*. Am I right?"

"Shut up."

By now my moron-meter was in the red, and I couldn't stand much more. "Listen if you guys want to be Alec's personal Secret Service, that's fine with me—but until you catch me red-handed trying to mess with him, stay out of my airspace!"

"Fair enough," said Moose, and stepped aside.

I shouldered Brett out of my way, and although he threw

a clump of wet sand at my back, I refused to let him provoke me.

"It'll only be a matter of time, Mercer," he shouted after me. "The truth is out there!"

My father cornered me in the kitchen the next morning before I left for school. "I want to talk about the message I got from your vice principal yesterday."

"I thought we talked last night." Actually I got out of having to discuss it by asking him to help me with math. I did need the help, and he was so pleased that I had asked him for anything that he forgot about the phone message from Mr. Greene (which luckily didn't give a clue as to why he had called). We had a good time, believe it or not, doing algebra together. Then, when the work was done, I guess he didn't have the heart to talk to me about Greene. I did hear him and Mom worry-talking, though, later at night when they thought I was asleep.

Dad poured himself a bowl of cereal. "I plan to call him back as soon as I get into work."

"Good. He likes it when people are prompt." I burned my fingers as I pulled my waffle from the toaster, and grimaced, shaking the pain out of my hand. My mom had already left for work, so they couldn't double-team me, but Dad was doing fine on his own.

"Are you in some sort of trouble, Jared? What's going

on in school? Have you done something we should know about?"

In social studies, we'd been learning about McCarthyism—you know—how back in the fifties some senators whose shorts got too tight decided that everyone who picked their nose the wrong way was a Communist. They formed a committee and began to ask people all kinds of questions like, "Are you now, or have you ever been a Communist?" Sort of like the questions my dad was asking now. Some people got really good at not answering.

"Have you done something wrong, Jared?"

"Not that I recall."

"Is there a reason why Mr. Greene would be calling us?"

"Not that I know of."

"What about your friends? Have they been getting into any trouble?"

"You want me to name names?"

He stared at me, like he so often did, in that state of parental confusion. It was Tyson who saved me.

"Mr. Greene was probably calling about me," Tyson said as he came into the kitchen. "He said he would call to see how I was doing with my new foster family." Tyson took my waffle. "So how am I doing?"

Dad relaxed. He was much more at ease with Tyson lately than he was with me. "Aside from eating us out of house and home, you're doing fine." Then he said his standard good-bye, and left.

"I really don't like lying to my parents," I told Tyson after my father was gone.

"Hey, what use am I if I don't teach you some bad habits?" he said.

"Anyway," I reminded him, "it won't hold up very long. He'll call Greene back, and I'll get my butt kicked halfway to China."

"Naah," Tyson said. "Your dad's not a butt-kicker, and anyway, he's not going to punish you for something you didn't do."

I wasn't so sure about that. I knew I had broken my parents' trust before. Would they believe me now, or would the weight of everyone else's suspicion sway them? When the Shadow Club was brought to justice the first time, they had taken away all my privileges—TV, video games, time with friends, time *anywhere* unsupervised. Gradually they had begun to give those things back, but they still withheld the most important thing of all: their trust. I had always taken it for granted that a parent's trust was a right, not a privilege.

As I pondered my own parents' faith in me, there was a knock at the door. I opened the door to see a kid standing there. A kid with a crew cut. It took me a few seconds to realize that it was Alec. Then it occurred to me that his little run-in with the Lunar Glue would leave him like that. I took a step back, almost expecting him to sock me or something, but that's not what he had in mind. He had a new look on his face. Yes, I could see anger there, but now there was something else, too, on top of the anger and resentment. It was fear.

"I want to know what I have to do to get you to stop," he said.

Tyson came in from the kitchen, took a few moments to gauge the situation, and slipped out the back door, realizing this was between just me and Alec.

"Why don't you come in," I said to him.

"Why? Is there an anvil hanging over the door?"

I backed up and opened the door wide to show him there was nothing about to fall on his head. Then he stepped in. I hurried to the kitchen.

"Want a waffle?" I asked him, fumbling with the package of frozen waffles.

"Not hungry."

"The haircut kinda suits you," I said, and then grimaced, realizing how dumb it was to say it.

"No, it doesn't," he said. "My cheeks are too big. I look like a chipmunk with a crew cut. What is it going to take to make you stop?" he said again.

This was a white flag of surrender, and as much as his arrogant nature irked me, I was even more bothered to see him defeated.

"You've got it wrong, Alec," I told him. "I'm not the enemy."

"Then what are you?" he said. "Because you're definitely not a friend."

I put my hands in my pockets. He was right, I wasn't a friend, but that really wasn't my fault.

"You don't have friends, Alec," I told him. "You have subjects, and servants."

"You wish you had a tenth of the respect that I had, but you don't, and that's why you hate me, isn't it? That and Cheryl."

"Leave Cheryl out of this." Then I leaned against the counter and took a deep breath. He was trying to draw me in, to make me angry, but I wasn't falling for that.

"Listen," I said, "maybe this was the last prank. Maybe, just maybe, the person who did it has realized it's gone too far, and they feel sorry they did it."

Alec stared at me, his eyes cold, unbelieving.

"And maybe they don't."

No matter how hard I tried, I couldn't help but face his angry distrust with matching defiance. "I guess we'll just have to wait and see, won't we."

A
Bitter Pill

I WAS CALLED INTO Mr. Greene's office right after lunch.

There were several chairs in Mr. Greene's office: a plush comfortable one for setting kids' minds at ease, a beanbag for less formal counseling sessions . . . and then there was the old wooden chair; a worn-out, high-backed, dark monster with wide armrests. Kids called it the "Electric Chair." This was the chair he had positioned in front of his desk when I was escorted into his office that morning.

"Come in, Jared. Have a seat," he said.

I sat down in the uncomfortable chair, figuring I would hear the same old stuff about how he thought I was the center of all local evil, but all he said was: "I like your shirt."

I looked down to notice that this was the same shirt I had worn on the days when Alec had commented on my shirt as well.

"I like your tie," I said to him. "Have you spoken to my parents yet?"

"We've been missing each other's calls." And then he sat there and just stared at me.

"Listen, is this important, because I'm missing English class."

"I will ask you this once," he said, "and I expect an honest answer."

"Sure."

"Did you put a skunk in Alec Smartz's minivan?"

"No, I did not," I said as directly as I could.

He leaned back in his chair, with a slight look of satisfaction on his face. "You might want to think about your answer." And then he reached into his drawer, pulled out a tiny plastic bag, and tossed it on his desk. At first I thought the bag was empty, but then I saw something in it—something small—something round and blue. It was a shirt button that looked very familiar. I looked down at the shirt I was wearing—the button was identical to my shirt buttons, and when I reached up to my collar, I found that the top button was missing. Suddenly I felt the hardness of the Electric Chair, and I knew what Mr. Greene's look of satisfaction was all about. It was the look of an executioner preparing to throw the switch.

"Do you know where this button was found?" he asked.

I shook my head.

"It was found on Alec Smartz's driveway—right near the spot where his van was parked that night." He reached out and took the button away from me. "Maybe you'd like to re-consider your answer."

I could only stammer, because I knew that no matter what I said, it would sound like a lie.

"Don't you have anything to say for yourself?"

"It's not my button," I said weakly, but we both knew that it had to be mine. The question was, how had it gotten there? I had never *been* on Alec Smartz's driveway.

"I'm going to give you one final chance, Jared," he said with the patience of someone completely sure of himself. "I'd like to put an end to this situation by tomorrow. Other-wise, it might get ugly."

But I wasn't listening to him anymore. I was thinking about that button. There were only two possibilities: either Alec was lying about where he found the button . . . or some-one had intentionally put it there for Alec to find.

But who? I thought. Who could have gotten that button? Then it dawned on me, in growing disbelief, that there was only one person in this school who had access to my shirts.

When I got home that afternoon, Tyson was already there, sitting in the living room with his headphones on, blasting his ears with one of my CDs. I pulled his headphones off, and his eyes snapped open.

"Hey, what gives?" he asked.

I wanted to grab him and shake him. I wanted to accuse him right there and pass judgment on him the way Greene had passed judgment on me, but I had done that once before to Tyson, hadn't I? I had beaten him silly, convinced that he was the one pulling the deadly pranks last fall, but I had been dead wrong. Maybe Greene was ready to throw the switch on me, but I wasn't going to do that to Tyson. No matter what I suspected, he deserved the benefit of my doubt.

I took a deep breath to steady myself, and said, "How do you like my shirt?"

He looked at me like I was nuts. "It's OK," he said.

"Notice anything wrong with it?"

He looked at my chest and pointed to it. "You got some mustard there." I looked down, and he dragged his finger up across my face.

"Gets 'em every time!" he said. "Nyuk, nyuk, nyuk."

I pushed his hand away, and he finally realized that this wasn't a laughing matter. "What's your problem today, huh?"

"Remember when you said you hated me?"

He rolled his eyes. "Are we going to go through that again?"

"Do you hate me enough to get me suspended? Do you hate me enough to get me thrown out of school?"

He sat up, and answered me with the same directness I answered Mr. Greene.

"No," he said, "I don't. I hate you enough to take the extra hamburger at dinner, so you don't get seconds."

"Do you hate me enough to plant evidence on Alec's driveway?"

"Are you accusing me of something?" He started to get that red-in-the-face look he always got when someone lit his microscopic fuse.

"I'm just asking." I watched him closely, trying to gauge the truth in his answer.

"No. I didn't." He thought for a moment, then said, "There was a time when I hated you more than anything, and there are still times when I want to hate you, but I just can't—and unless you do something *really* stupid, I probably never will." Then he stormed across the room, and turned to face me again, but he kept his distance. "You're my best friend, OK? There, I said it. The guy who ruined my life is now my best friend. Pretty pathetic, huh?"

"No, it's not," I said, feeling like a total jerk. There was no doubting his honesty about it.

"It *is* pathetic," Tyson insisted, "because I know you're not really my friend at all."

"What?"

"You feel sorry for me . . . you feel *guilty* for what you did, but you really don't *like* me."

"That's not true!"

"Prove it," he said.

I opened my mouth to speak, but nothing came out. I couldn't prove to Tyson that I was his friend, any more than I could prove my innocence to Greene.

"We'll never be on equal ground," said Tyson, "unless I

ruin your life, and then turn around and save it, like you did to me. Then if you can tell me we're friends, that's when I'll believe you."

I don't know if Greene had spoken to my parents, because they didn't talk to me about it. That, I think, was as unsettling as if I had been punished for something I didn't do. Still, I tried to convince myself that this was over; that three dirty tricks was the charm that would break the spell, and whoever was doing it would slink back into whatever hole they crawled out of. But, like I said, something was set loose in our school, and Alec, simply by being Alec, kept making himself the target. But what he did next—his own little counterattack—was as unforgivable as any of the pranks pulled against him. It wasn't a prank that he pulled, but it was despicable nonetheless. It was as mean-spirited as it was self-serving, but all it served to do was feed the fires of resentment.

It happened on the day of the candidates' televised statements. About a year ago, our school had converted the audiovisual office into a television studio of sorts, and the school got wired for closed-circuit TV. This year, for the first time, each presidential candidate had recorded a five-minute campaign speech that would be televised throughout the entire ninth grade. I watched in social studies class—a class I didn't share with either Cheryl or Alec. Tommy Nickols came on first. The highlight of his rather dull speech was a top ten list—the top ten reasons why he should be voted in. It was supposed to be very funny, but was in fact so unfunny that people were laughing hysterically by the end of it. Unfortunately, they were laughing *at* Tommy and not *with* him. Next came Katrina's speech, which seemed like one long, rambling telephone conversation with herself. Cheryl's speech was masterful, as I knew it would be, and then came Alec's. No one, not even me, was prepared for what he did.

"Hello, friends and classmates," his speech began. "It is with great regret that I share with you some information I discovered just the other day. Something that every one of you has a right to know." We all listened closely, wondering what sort of bombshell Alec had to drop. Like everything else he did, it fell like a nuke.

"The video you are about to see was filmed a few days ago," he said on the TV. "I ask that you all watch closely." Suddenly the image of Alec changed to a handheld video shot of a place I recognized—a place filled with old, crumbling boats. *Oh no*, I said to myself, *he didn't* . . . but unfortunately he did. The video had been edited down to less than a minute, and within that minute, I saw Tyson and myself climb up in the hole of the tugboat, and then Abbie, Darren, O. P., Jason, and Randall. Finally the camera zoomed in to catch Cheryl, the image grainy and wobbly. She looked around, as if she was up to no good, and there the video ended. Alec came back on the screen. I slunk low in my chair.

"Several months ago," he said, "a group of seven kids terrorized this school, and they called themselves the Shadow Club. You thought they had been brought to justice. You thought they were sorry for what they had done, but you thought wrong. If that's the kind of person you want leading your class into high school, then vote for Cheryl whats-her-face. Otherwise you know where to cast your vote."

I didn't see it, but I hear their breakup was spectacular. Jodi Lattimer told me, and she was never one to gossip, so the source was reliable.

"Alec accused Cheryl of tearing down his posters," Jodi said, "and Cheryl called Alec more four-letter words than I knew existed. Some of them had, like, ten letters."

It was a breakup that could make record books, but this was about much more than that. Alec had incriminated us all with that video. Even though it showed nothing, really, it showed just enough to let everyone's imagination run rampant.

I went to the tugboat to be alone, to convince myself that there was a way to deal with this, and that I was strong enough to do it. I wasn't feeling strong at all, I was feeling weak, angry, and confused. That's when Cheryl showed up.

"Permission to come aboard?" she asked.

"Permission granted."

She climbed in through the hole in the hull, and we sat across from each other, as we had done so many times before in the old tree house. A winter storm had taken down that tree house this year, and most of its wood had been burned in her fireplace. Thinking about that bothered me more than I think it should have.

"Someone find me a bear so I can put it in Alec's minivan," she said.

"Careful—we might find ourselves on cable tonight."

She shook her head, furious at herself. "How could I have been so stupid to trust him? I'm never going to trust anyone ever again."

I laughed. "Now you sound like me." Then I took a long look at her. I could see how much she was hurting. "Don't worry," I told her, "he'll get his someday."

"Well, I hope he gets it soon." Then she drew up her knees, realizing what she was saying. There it was, that old resentment.

"You want him hurt as much as he hurt you," I said. "I mean, what he did was really nasty, it's OK to feel that way."

"Are you my guidance counselor now?"

I grinned. "Me, or Greene—take your pick."

Cheryl took a deep breath and let it out slowly. "Do you think he would have done it if he knew *why* we were all meeting . . . and if I hadn't laughed at him the other day?"

I fiddled with a nail that was sticking out of the hull. "Maybe, maybe not. You know him better than I do."

"That's what I thought." She considered it for a few moments and clenched her fists, still fighting her fury.

"I swore that I would never feel that way about anyone ever again," Cheryl said. "I swore I would never be so angry that I'd wish awful things on someone."

"Wishing and making it happen are two different things," I reminded her.

"Yeah, but sometimes wishes come true."

The Shadow Club might have been dead, but thanks to Alec Smartz it had risen from the grave. Everyone from Principal Diller to the cafeteria servers believed we were conspiring up a new reign of terror. Whether or not Alec realized what he did, he put the seven of us back in the center of attention.

I was in Greene's office first thing the next morning. I had expected it—he couldn't leave that incriminating video unanswered. Once I took my seat in the Electric Chair, he didn't waste any time beating around the bush.

"It was made very clear to you last October," he began, "that if the so-called Shadow Club was ever caught meeting again, it would be grounds for dismissal."

"You're going to expel us because we talked for five minutes? You don't even know what we talked about!"

"I have an idea."

"We were trying to figure out who's pulling tricks on Alec—ask the others—they'll tell you."

"I'm sure that's what they'll tell me," Greene said calmly, making it clear he wouldn't believe it, no matter who told him. "But the only thing I know for sure is that *you* called the meeting. That makes you the only one who's really in danger of being expelled."

"Fine! Then take me to Principal Diller! Maybe he'll listen to me!"

"No. I won't bother Principal Diller with you, because you're my problem, Jared. You've been my problem this entire school year, and I will make sure this is taken care of."

"Go ahead," I shouted. "Tell my parents I'm a delinquent. I'm sure you've told them already."

Greene sighed. "Your parents," he said, "are very defensive of you."

I wasn't expecting to hear that my parents would defend me in anything. While I grappled with what to make of that, there was a knock at the door, and a teacher poked her head inside. She stood with a girl who was upset about something that, mercifully, didn't involve me.

"Mr. Greene, could I have your help?" the teacher asked.

Reluctantly, Greene stood up from his desk. "I'm not done with you," Greene told me. "You wait right here, and think very carefully about your future in this school. When I get back I want to hear about your meeting, and about the pranks."

He strode out, closing the door behind him, leaving me with my thoughts . . . but when I looked at his desk, I realized he had left me alone with *his* thoughts, too. There, on his desk, was my file. For an instant I fought the urge to look at what he had written about me, but in the end, I reached over and flipped open the file with one finger, tilting my head to look at it, afraid he'd notice if I moved it. Although his handwriting was hard to read, one phrase in his latest report leaped out at me like a nasty jack-in-the-box—"deeply troubled," it said, "with sociopathic tendencies."

My first instinct was to laugh. Me? Troubled? I thought. I might have been *in trouble* from time to time. I might have done some pretty stupid things now and then, but it always seemed to me that my troubles were no deeper than a wading pool. My family life was okay, my frustrations were typical, I guess. Troubled? That was absolutely ridiculous. When I rebounded from my laughter, it was the second phrase that hit me hard—*sociopathic*. I wasn't quite certain what the word meant, but I had my suspicions. I found a fat dictionary on Mr. Greene's shelves, and pulled it down to look up the word.

"Sociopath," it said; "a person who lacks conscience, or moral responsibility."

I felt as if someone had just punched me in the stomach. I could feel the air squeeze out of my lungs, and I gasped to breathe it back in. "There's a word for people like you," Brett Whatley had said. Had he been sneaking a peek at my file, too? I sat back down in the Electric Chair, slamming the dictionary closed. Then I closed my eyes and reached down into myself—really deep down—to prove to myself that Greene was wrong, and just because he wrote it, it didn't make it so. I didn't have to go very deep at all to find the conscience Greene thought was so lacking in me. It was alive and well, but it was totally hidden from his view.

What Greene was doing to me was like a witch trial. Hundreds of years ago they used to try witches in a water test. They believed witches were made out of wood, and since wood floats, obviously a witch would float, too. If the person sank and drowned in the well, then obviously that person wasn't a witch. I felt myself sinking into the bottom of that well now—my life and everything I cared about slipping away. I wasn't about to let that happen. I was stronger than that—stronger than Greene—and it dawned on me exactly what I had to do.

Mr. Greene's supposed evidence of my crimes sat in a little plastic bag clipped to my file. The blue shirt button. I slipped it out of the bag and put it in my shirt pocket, then realized that it was easily found there. So, instead, I put it on my tongue and swallowed it. I could feel it going all the way down. The tips of my fingers and toes became numb, as if I had swallowed some pill instead of a button. Then I sat back down in the Electric Chair, just as Mr. Greene came back into the room and took his place across from me. I forced myself to stare him straight in the eye, unwavering, pretending to be in total control of myself, of the situation, and of him.

"I'm ready to listen, if you're ready to talk," he said.

"I have nothing to say to you." I forced a rudeness into my voice that I had never showed anyone before—much less an adult.

Greene was ready for this, as if he had been expecting it all along.

"How much longer do you think you can keep up the lies, Jared? It's only a matter of time before the truth surfaces. We already have your button and—"

"What button?"

He glanced down at the file, and the smug look on his face dissolved.

"All right, give it back."

Although I was feeling queasy—not from the button, but from the course I was choosing—I forced myself to grin.

"I don't know what you're talking about," I said very slowly, pretending to be in control, keeping my eyes locked onto his. I don't know, but maybe my own lurking discomfort coupled with that icy stare appeared suitably sociopathic to him, because he changed. He seemed a little bit smaller, and maybe even frightened.

"What are you trying to pull?" he asked.

But I kept that grin painted across my face, and suddenly

I realized that I was no longer *pretending* to be in control of the situation. I was.

"Maybe I did all of those things to Alec," I told Greene. "But you'll never prove it . . . because I'm too smart for you." Then I stood up, and strutted out of his office without looking back. If this was a witch trial, then I was not going to drown with a whimper, I would float in defiance. I would be the witch.

Shaditude

PLAYING THE BAD kid is hard work when it doesn't come naturally, but I was a quick study, and I was motivated. Tyson helped some. He was never really a bad kid himself—he was just kind of creepy—but he did understand what it took far better than I did. He treated it like a joke as he taught me the ins and outs of being unwholesome.

"This is the way you slouch in your chair," he said as we sat at the kitchen table. "You lean way far back from your desk."

I tried it.

"No," he said. "You're still too close. Your hands can still reach your schoolwork. You gotta slouch far enough away— maybe even tip your chair back a little bit—so that there is no way you can get to anything on your desk without major effort."

"Oh, I get it. It's kind of like your textbooks are repelling you."

"Exactly." He walked across the room and watched me

again. "Okay, the slouch is good. Now pretend I'm the teacher. What are you going to do?"

"I'm going to stare at you," I said. "Like I can see through you."

Tyson shook his head. Wrong answer.

"Naah. That might have worked for Greene, because he was trying to see through you first. With a teacher you want to look away."

So I tried looking away.

"No, not out of the window—then it seems like you're just daydreaming. You can't look down either. You have to pick a blank spot on the wall and look at it, so that it's very clear you're not looking at anything. Everyone has to know that you're doing it on purpose."

I took a deep breath and sighed. "Is all this really necessary?"

"Hey, you're the one who wants to look bad."

I went out before dark and bought some new clothes. "Bad" clothes. Shirts and pants that had the ragged and rude look of defiance. When I got home, I modeled them for Tyson. That's when he started to get worried.

"What's the matter?" I asked. "Did I get the wrong clothes?"

"No," Tyson answered. "It's just that . . . I don't know . . . You don't look like yourself, Jared."

I turned to look at the mirror on Tyson's closet door. He was right. I looked like my own evil twin.

"Well, this is how I look now."

He shifted his shoulders uncomfortably. "Why do you want to do this?" he asked.

But I didn't tell him. I had my reasons, but right now I couldn't share them with anyone.

When I left Tyson's room, I ran into my mom in the hallway. Mom, always to the point said, "I don't like when you dress that way, Jared."

I wasn't surprised that she didn't like it. What surprised me was the way she said it—like I had dressed this way before.

"It's what everyone's wearing."

"You're not everyone," she said, then added, "you want to dress like that, you wash those clothes yourself. I won't do it."

I wore the clothes to school the next day, and the effect was instantaneous. I got double takes from everyone in the hallway—kids and teachers alike. I raised eyebrows in every class as I slouched and looked off toward nothing, wearing my attitude like a heavy cologne that filled the air around me.

Shaditude, I called it—the attitude everyone thought the leader of the Shadow Club would have.

It really infuriated Greene—and as much as that scared me, there was some satisfaction in it as well. Suddenly *he* was the paranoid one instead of me. During passing that first day, Jodi Lattimer tried to give me some notes that I had missed while receiving Greene's third degree. Greene seemed to appear out of nowhere, staring at Jodi, like we were doing something illegal. "What's this all about?" he snapped. We both looked at him as if he was from Mars.

"Tell me about that hat, Miss Lattimer."

Jodi was wearing her denim baseball cap—this time it was forward instead of backward. On the front in bright orange were the letters "TSC."

"What's to tell?" she said calmly. "My father belongs to the Tennis and Squash Center. We have a bunch of them."

It took me a second to realize what Greene was thinking. That "TSC" could also stand for The Shadow Club.

"Are you going to expel her because of the hat?" I asked.

He threw me a gaze meant to chill me. I knew he had scheduled me a parent conference for the end of the week. He was making all these noises about suspension and expulsion, and yeah, it bothered me—an expulsion followed you wherever you went—but Greene's X-ray gaze didn't intimidate me anymore, because I knew it wasn't going to see through anything.

There must be some fourth law of thermodynamics. Along with the law of conservation of energy, there must be some kind of conservation of oddity, keeping the world in balance. It only figured that as I began to resemble a mother's worst nightmare, someone else's act began to clean up.

I came home from school during that first week of the

Shaditude to find some strange kid rummaging through my refrigerator for food. One of Tyson's friends, I figured, which was bizarre, because Tyson never brought home friends. I didn't know he had any. I was about to ask if I could help him find something, then I remembered my Shaditude, and said, "You take something, you pay for it, dude."

The kid turned around to reveal a familiar face in an entirely unfamiliar package.

"Hi, Jared."

It wasn't a friend of Tyson's at all. It was Tyson himself. His hair, which had always been long and stringy, was cut short, with a smooth line along the back of his neck. He had even shaved those goat hairs on his neck that might someday become a beard.

"Uh . . . nice 'do," I said, still reeling from the sight. What's the word for something that's a total logical inconsistency? An oxymoron. Yeah, that's what Tyson was. "Tyson McGaw" and "clean cut" did not go together in the same sentence without causing a major short circuit—like the one I had now as I gaped at him. Actually, oxy-moron was a better description of me at that moment—a *moron* whose brain wasn't getting enough *oxy*gen.

"You like it?" he asked, running his hand through what was left of his hair.

"Yeah, sure," I said, still wading through recovery. "It'll blow everyone away."

"Well," he said, "I figured if you could be your own evil

twin, I could be my own un-psycho twin." He grabbed his jacket and headed for the door.

"You're off in a hurry," I said, and laughed. "What, have you got a date or something?" I meant it as a joke, but Tyson wasn't laughing.

"As a matter of fact, I do."

Right about now, the signpost up ahead was beginning to read "The Twilight Zone," but I couldn't exactly say why. *Yes, you can say why,* my get-real voice told me. *It's because Tyson is Tyson and the earth spins out of orbit if he suddenly has friends and short hair and a girlfriend and—*

"Who's the lucky girl?"

"Jodi Lattimer."

"No way."

"Yeah—we're going out to Dairy Queen for some ice cream, and just to hang out, y'know."

"That's not exactly a date," I informed him, even though I knew it technically was.

He shrugged. "Call it whatever you want."

Then I noticed something else about him. He was wearing one of my shirts.

"Who gave you permission to put that on?" This time it wasn't Shaditude—it was all me.

"Well, you're not wearing your old stuff anymore."

"It doesn't fit you anyway, it just hangs on you on account of you don't have any pecs."

Tyson took it as an insult, which I suppose it was. "I got pecs!" he said, pushing out his chest. "I've been working out—I've got pecs up the wazoo!"

The fact that, yes, my shirt actually *did* fit him wasn't really the point. I wasn't exactly sure what the point was, only that I was truly annoyed.

Then something struck me, and suddenly Tyson looked all different to me again.

"How long have you been wearing my shirts?"

He shrugged. "I tried one on yester—" And his face changed again, like he was a regular chameleon, the minute he realized why I was asking. He thought for a moment, his face going granite hard, his lips pursing into a tight little hole in his face. "Well, of course, there was the time last week when I wore your shirt and popped a button on Alec Smartz's driveway. Nobody knew but me and the skunk."

Sometimes—not often, but sometimes my brain turns into Play-Doh, and I find my mouth opening and closing as I try to squeeze an intelligent thought through the doh-matic press.

"Duh . . . Are you serious? You're not serious, right? Are you kidding? Was that a confession? You're kidding, right?"

Tyson shook his head. "If you have to ask, then you don't deserve an answer."

And he left, leaving me on the doorstep to press my Play-Doh.

By the next day I had reached the inevitable conclusion that Tyson was just being Tyson, and probably had nothing to do with the button. At first I wondered how he even knew about it, but by now everyone knew about that button. Still some residual suspicion remained, like the smell of bug spray in the summer. One minute I was suspicious of him, and the next I felt all guilty about feeling that way.

Between classes, I found Jodi Lattimer at her locker. I approached her as though I was just making friendly conversation, but I had a reason for looking for her. Two reasons, actually.

"Hi, Jodi," I said.

"Hi, Jared."

"So . . . I hear you and Tyson went to the Dairy Queen."

"Yeah," she said as if it was nothing. "And next week we're going to the movies."

"Good," I said. "That's great. So you actually like him."

"Yeah. Is that so hard to believe?"

"No, not at all." Now this was getting awkward. "It's just . . . it's just that Tyson's been through a lot, y'know. I just don't want to see him hurt."

"Sounds like you're jealous."

Well, maybe I was and maybe I wasn't. I hadn't quite sorted that out yet, but I was pretty certain that jealousy—if there was any—was secondary to my genuine concern for Tyson. At least the concern I felt when I wasn't feeling suspicious of him. Anyway, the last thing Tyson needed was a game of hormonal tetherball with a girl who took it too lightly.

"Just don't toy with him, OK?"

"What, are you his father now?"

"He doesn't have a father—in case you didn't know."

"So I've heard."

This wasn't going well, but before we escalated into the "fine-be-that-way" mode, Jodi disarmed.

"Listen . . . Tyson can take care of himself," she said. "And he does it pretty well." Then she looked me over. "Nice clothes," she said, in a way that made it completely unclear whether she liked my new clothes, or whether she was just being sarcastic.

"Yeah, well, it's a look," I said. "Anyway, Tyson's not the reason why I wanted to talk to you. I wanted to see if I could get your hat."

"My hat?"

"Yeah," I said offhandedly, trying to hide how much I really wanted it. "It's kind of cool."

"Why don't you just go to the Tennis and Squash Center and get your own?"

I pulled a bill out of my pocket. "I'll give you ten dollars for it."

"Suit yourself." She took my money, pulled the hat from her head, and handed it to me. I suppose ten bucks warranted no questions asked. Or maybe she just didn't care.

Regardless, anyone who saw me wearing the hat, even if they knew where it really came from, would know what TSC meant for me. It was exactly what I needed to make my bad-kid illusion complete.

For lunch that day I didn't go out to Solerno's, I stayed in the cafeteria. I positioned my TSC hat just right, then I found a kid who wouldn't give me any trouble, and just pushed my way in front of him in line.

"Hey!" he complained.

I turned to him and stared. "You got a problem?"

He backed down and said nothing.

Quite a few kids noticed my behavior, and I took note of which kids were intimidated, which kids were annoyed, and which kids suddenly seemed to gravitate toward me, impressed by my new mean image. During the next couple of days, it was those impressed kids that I made a point of nodding to, and giving a friendly rap on the shoulder as I passed by, like they were all my new best friends.

Mitchell Bartok, a kid so tough he must have worn leather diapers as a baby, made a point of sitting at my lunch table on the third day of the Shaditude. We bad-mouthed teachers together and said some rude things about various girls we saw around the cafeteria. I pretended that I knew something about Harleys, and suddenly he was telling me his life story. Then, as the lunch bell rang, I turned to him and said: "Hey, Mitchell, all that stuff you did to Alec was pretty funny."

But he looked at me cluelessly. "I thought *you* did all that stuff."

"Yeah . . . yeah sure," I said. "Just kidding you."

When he was gone I opened my notebook and crossed him off my list of suspects.

Each day, when I got home, I went straight into the bathroom and peeled off my new self, like a full body mask. Then I stepped into a hot shower and scrubbed myself, feeling dirty, but knowing that the worst dirt wouldn't come off with soap. All those nasty things I said and did to build my new false image, all the tricks I was playing on kids like Mitch Bartok to ferret out the truth. I guess what bothered me most was that everyone seemed to believe my bad-kid act. I mean, I'm not a great actor, but in this case it wasn't hard to become what they made me. And it scared me . . . because part of me liked it—just as part of me had liked the secret power I wielded as the leader of the Shadow Club, back when we were at our worst. And so each day I didn't stop scrubbing until I could find myself underneath, and remembered that I liked my real self a whole lot more.

And then there were my parents, who seemed to have invoked a ten-foot-pole policy with me. Not physical distance, but emotional. I knew that Greene was preparing for a big meeting with them next week—and yet my parents said nothing to me about that, or any of the things Greene must have been telling them. That scared me more than their House un-American Activities questioning. It's like they were so worried, they chose to stick their heads in the ground, and broke off all communication with me. I mean, what if I really was up to something terrible? How could they not get after me for the way I was acting—even if it was just an act? I could forgive my parents for prying too much, but it was harder to forgive them for not prying at all.

Jodi showed up at our house that Friday—the end of my first week of Shaditude. She walked in the front door like she owned the place—serves me right for leaving it open. I was lying on my bed, trying not to think of anything in particular. I used to be very good at that, but in recent months my thoughts were way too focused much of the time—usually on things I didn't enjoy thinking about. I was tossing that seashell of mine up into the air, trying to see how high I could get it without actually hitting the ceiling. My mom once told me it was a very "Zen" thing to do—whatever that means. With my headphones blasting music, a freight train could have come through the house and I wouldn't have known. Naturally, when I looked up and saw Jodi there at my bedroom door I was startled, lost my concentration and the shell came down, hitting me in the face. I took the headphones off and the blaring music became tinny and distant.

"I'm looking for Tyson," she said.

"He's not here," I told her. "I'll tell him you came by."

But she didn't go just yet. She glanced at the ballistic seashell that had done its damage and now lay innocently on my bed. "You're supposed to do that with a baseball, aren't you?" she asked. "Y'know—toss it up and down."

I shrugged looking at the shell. "Baseballs don't break."

"Isn't that the point?"

"I don't know," I said. "Where's the challenge if nothing's at risk?"

"Wow," she said. "Deep."

She looked around, never stepping into the room. I felt like I was under a microscope again. "See anything interesting?"

"Your room's not what I expected."

I looked around. My desk was a mess of schoolwork, but otherwise, the room was pretty neat. There was a poster of Carl Lewis bursting through an Olympic finish line, because I'm a runner; a poster of a Ferrari Testarosa, because I like cars; and a poster of supermodel Lorna LeBlanc because . . . well, just because. All in all, my room was nothing out of the ordinary.

"What did you expect?" I asked. "Pipe bombs and hate literature?"

"Nah, you're too smart for that," she said, and then added far too seriously for my taste, "You'd keep that stuff much better hidden." She glanced at the shell, which had found its way back into my fidgety hands. "So what do you hear when you put that thing to your ear, the sea?"

"I hear the voices of all the kids I had to kill, because they saw my room." I thought she might laugh at that, but she didn't give me so much as a chuckle. "Yeah," I told her, "I do hear the sea and it reminds me of all the bad stuff that happened in October."

"If it were me," Jodi said, "I'd never put it to my ear."

"I like being reminded," I told her, "so I'll never do it again." I could sense that she didn't really believe me, but I didn't care who believed me anymore. "If you're dating Tyson, why are you so interested in me?"

Jodi shrugged. "A few months ago you almost got him killed, yet now he talks about you like you're God at fourteen, so I guess I was just curious." She backed out of the doorjamb, preparing to leave. "Tell Tyson I stopped by," she said, and she pointed at my eye, which was still aching from where the shell hit. "And you better get some ice on that, unless a black eye is part of your new look."

After she left, I put the shell in a drawer instead of back on the shelf.

If it were me, I'd never put it to my ear.

Maybe she was right. I had a world full of reminders already. There were enough people looking back at what I had done. That was one club I didn't need to be a part of anymore.

Alec Blows Up

I SHOULD HAVE been the town hero for what happened next, but when you're pegged, you're pegged, and if people want to, they can see the worst of intentions in the best of acts. I spent the next lunch period alone in the library. It was one of those cold windy days when few kids would brave the walk to Solerno's. Most everyone was down in the cafeteria, and that's not where I wanted to be. I didn't want to see Alec, didn't want to think about him, so I sat studying world history, idly wondering if it could teach me anything about how to avoid bad situations. Unfortunately, all history taught me was that bad situations tended to get worse and worse until an awful lot of people were dead.

That's when O. P. sort of staggered into the library. The worried look was plastered as prominently across her face as the campaign fliers in the hallways. She sat down across from me, not saying anything, waiting for me to ask the obvious question.

"What's up, O. P.?"

"Somebody slipped this into my backpack," she said, and handed me a piece of paper. Scrawled on it, in a handwriting I could barely read, were the words:

We're on your side.

"Who's 'we'?" I asked.

She shook her head. "I don't know . . . but that's not all." She looked around, like a spy about to hand me some crucial microfilm, and then flipped the paper over to reveal that the note had been scribbled on a medical form—the kind that the school nurse kept in her office for every student. This one has been filled out, and the name on the form was Alec Smartz.

"Someone gave you Alec's medical info?" I asked, not quite getting it.

"I don't know what it means," she said, looking more worried than the time she forgot to study for a science exam. "But I'm beginning to think that maybe you were right about things starting all over again . . . and that maybe this note wasn't meant just for me—maybe it was meant for the whole Shadow Club.

"But what does it have to do with Alec's medical record?"

O. P. just shrugged.

I read through Alec's medical form three times—like I

said, I'm not that great with details—but on the third pass I caught it.

At first I refused to believe that anyone would stoop so low, but the more I thought about it, the more I realized that only one thing on that sheet of paper could be used against Alec. O. P. must have seen it in my face.

"What is it?"

I handed back the piece of paper, feeling the tiny hairs on my arms and legs begin to rise, even though the library was oppressively warm.

"Alec's allergic to penicillin."

I bolted out of there before I could see O. P.'s reaction, and raced down the hall, bursting down the stairwell, taking four steps at a time. I knocked a kid down as I crashed into the first-floor hallway. The cafeteria was at the far end, and as I ran toward it, putting all my speed and strength into my legs, I felt the same sense of futility I had four months earlier when I watched Austin Pace race barefoot toward a jagged pile of rocks lying in wait for him. Back then I knew I wasn't fast enough to catch up with him, to stop him. That's exactly how I felt now.

I ran into the cafeteria door with the full force of my body. Someone caught behind the door yelped, but I never saw him. Instead I scoured the crowded room for Alec. He was in the far corner, surrounded by his close friends and bodyguards: an unlikely inner circle that ranged from the brawny likes of Moose SanGiorgio, to the weaselly Calvin Horner, who was responsible for Alec's nomination, and was probably the spy who took that video. Then I saw Alec reach for a bottle of orange soda. He had given up Dr Pepper, and anything that reminded him of it, for obvious reasons. He probably assumed drinking from a bottle was safer than from a cup—after all, anyone can mess with a cup—but was he cautious enough to listen for that telltale hiss as the soda was opened to make sure it hadn't been tampered with?

I pushed my way through crowds, knocking over kids in my way. The sound of crashing trays gained everyone's attention, but I couldn't worry about that now. Weaving between tables and leaping over chairs like a hurdler, I finally reached him. I tried to slow down, but lost my balance, nailing my gut against the side of the table. Alec had his head tilted back guzzling the orange soda, and I reached out and slammed it out of his hands.

"Hey, what the . . ."

It splashed all over the kids around him before landing on the floor, spilling out on the green linoleum.

"Are you nuts?" Alec yelled. "Have you totally lost your mind?"

I didn't have time for stupid questions. "*Was it flat?*" I asked.

"Huh?"

"The soda—*was it flat when you opened it?*"

He just looked at me blankly, so I got down on my hands and knees, running my fingers through the sticky orange liquid. I wasn't sure what I was searching for . . . maybe undissolved granules within the soda that fizzed between my fingers.

I grabbed for the bottle that still spun on the floor. Nothing inside but a few drops of soda. I drank it. It tasted normal, untainted. I took a deep and welcomed breath of relief.

When I looked up, about a dozen kids were staring down at me. For a moment I locked eyes with Austin Pace, who was now a part of Alec's entourage. What's that old expression? My enemy's enemy is my friend? The two of them must have been getting along famously.

"He's insane!" said Austin. "He's gone completely off the deep end!"

"I don't think he was all there to begin with," said Alec.

My camouflage pants had now absorbed enough of the soda to be orange from the knees down, and my hands were still dripping the stuff. I came to the sudden realization that in my entire life I had never looked quite so stupid. I wished I could have been anywhere else in the world right then.

"Are you having fun?" Alec asked.

I stood up, trying to avoid eye contact with the kids around me, and reached into my pocket, pulling out a crumpled dollar bill. "Sorry," I said, handing him the dollar. "Buy yourself a new soda."

He threw the bill back at me. "I don't want your stupid money. I want to know what this is all about."

I opened my mouth to tell him, but quickly shut it again. I had overreacted—I knew that now. I had drawn the wrong conclusion from that medical report, and I looked silly enough without trying to explain the details of my stupidity. "I just thought there was something wrong with your soda, that's all."

"I don't like your mind games, Mercer."

"Yeah, get lost," said Austin.

"Yeah," echoed Brett Whatley, who stood with his arms crossed, trying to fill his role as bodyguard. Alec sat back down, dismissing me like a fly he had swatted away. "Better clean that up," he said, chowing down on his chili. But getting back down on all fours again was an indignity I wasn't going to endure. I turned, fully prepared to make my escape from this painful situation . . . until I heard something that stopped me dead in my tracks.

"Ugh!" Alex said. "What do they make this chili out of, anyway? Cigarette butts and coffee grounds?"

I turned back to see Moose take a taste of his own chili. "Mine tastes fine."

Alec took a second spoonful. "Barely edible," he said.

I moved toward them again, and this time dipped my finger into his chili, and tasted it.

Moose got up, ready to hurl me through the wall like a

nightclub bouncer. But Moose was the least of my concerns now . . . because Alec's chili had a distinctly bitter, chalky taste . . .

"Alec, how allergic are you to penicillin?"

Suddenly he began to take me far more seriously than he had a moment before. "Why?"

But I already could tell that he was starting to feel uncomfortable, as though he had a slight fever coming on. His face was beginning to flush.

"We've got to get you out of here! We've got to get you to the nurse's office!"

I could see in his face the moment that it clicked. His eyes were panicked and accusing.

"What did you do?"

There wasn't time to explain. His lips were beginning to get puffy. I knew what an allergic reaction was like. I was allergic to bees. I had been stung three times in my life, and each time my reaction got worse. Now they were more dangerous for me than a rattlesnake or black widow spider bite. There was an adrenaline injector in the office with my name on it. I didn't know if a shot of adrenaline worked on penicillin the way it worked on bee stings, but the nurse would have to know.

Alec began to walk toward the cafeteria door, his eyes swelling in tears of fear. He wasn't walking fast enough, so I grabbed his arm and pulled him. He didn't shake me off—he let me part the gawking onlookers, who were probably wondering what on earth that maniac Jared Mercer was up to.

By the time we got to the office, Alec's face was blotchy and he looked as though someone was slowly pumping him up with air. It wouldn't be long before his whole body became one huge, red, swollen hive. I could feel him quivering as I pulled him past the counter toward the nurse's office.

"You're not allowed back here," said the school secretary.

Ignoring her, we burst into the nurse's office, and miraculously, the nurse was actually there, in the middle of lunch. She looked up with linguini hanging out of her mouth.

"Allergic reaction!" I shouted. "Penicillin."

"My God." She was quick to react. She called out to the secretary to dial 911, and Alec settled into a chair, his knees shaky. I wasn't sure whether that was part of the reaction, or just his fear. "How much did he ingest? How long ago."

"A lot—just now. You need an adrenaline injector? Mine's here, somewhere."

I tried to find it, but ended up knocking over a shelf full of medical stuff.

"Go talk to the emergency operator. Tell them what you told me." Then she pushed me out the door.

It didn't take very long for word of this to get around school. Just about everyone knew about the "incident" by the time the ambulance arrived and took Alec away.

"Everyone knows you did it," taunted Brett Whatley,

who sat behind me in science. "Just because you chickened out at the last moment and tried to stop it doesn't mean you're not guilty." And I knew the whole school felt the same way. After all, who else but the person who did it could have known that his food was spiked with penicillin? And me, with my new set of clothes, and attitude—how could they draw any other conclusion? I couldn't find O. P. to get me off the hook with the note she had gotten, and I figured she was too scared to get anywhere near this now.

I kept looking around to see if there was anyone fidgeting—someone feeling the weight of the guilt for what they had done, or someone irritated that I got all the credit. I had compiled about fifteen possible suspects in my notebook. Half of them I had already crossed off, of the other half I was still uncertain.

There was nothing to do but run. I didn't want to talk to anybody, I didn't want to see anybody, and although I didn't want to be alone with my own thoughts either, I figured by running I could outdistance them a little bit. If I could focus my attention on the pounding of my feet and the rhythm of my breathing, maybe I could stop thinking for a few minutes. I cut class, ditching a math test, and took to the streets. I didn't know where I was going and didn't follow my usual path, I just ran. I ran down Pine Street, where there was nothing but winter-dead sycamores. I ran past Solerno's, empty at this off-hour of the afternoon. I ran to the marina toward the Ghosties, but didn't want to go into that old boat graveyard, so I turned around and doubled back, taking the road that wound around the jagged shoreline. I just kept weaving, for what seemed like hours.

I could take a lie-detector test, I thought, and prove to them I was telling the truth. But I had to face the fact that nothing I said would prove anything, because people beat lie-detector tests. Sociopaths could lie without a blip, so it wouldn't prove my innocence, it would only confirm what Greene already thought he knew about me. I began to wonder why we were made so people couldn't get into your head. Outside of your own thoughts, there was no such thing as truth, only what other people thought was true.

I was so wrapped up in my own thoughts I didn't even notice the car pulling up beside me, until the window rolled down and I heard the driver's voice.

"Get in."

It was so flat, so void of any familiar emotion, I didn't recognize it at first. I turned sharply, almost stumbling, and saw my father. I heard the power locks pop up. "Get in," he said again.

I stopped running, and the car slowed to a stop a few yards ahead of me. For a moment I considered turning around and running off in the other direction. I could ditch into the woods—he wouldn't be able to follow me then. And then I thought, How long has he been driving through town, looking for me? Our town is pretty big—the thought of my father driving for hours until finding me made me move toward the car, pull open the door, and get in.

I sat in the passenger seat without looking at him, closed the door, and we drove off. He started to wind through the outskirts of town, making turns without using his signal. It scared me, because my father wears a seat belt, goes the speed limit, and he always, *always* signals. His life is all safety and stability. That's probably why he got into selling homeowners' insurance. Everything has to be protected. He took the business with the Shadow Club pretty hard last October. I guess it drove him nuts that he couldn't protect me from me.

"Your mother and I have been called in to see your principal tomorrow," he finally said. "But I'm sure you already know that."

"I can explain—"

"BE QUIET!" he shouted. It caught me completely by surprise. He had raised his voice to me before, but never so suddenly—never with such rage behind his words. For an instant I thought he might hit me, even though he had never hit me before. *"You are not here to talk, you are here to listen. Do you understand me?"*

I nodded. "Yes, sir." I couldn't remember ever calling him "sir" before.

"Your mother and I know about what's been happening to that Alec kid. We know about the incident today, too."

I opened my mouth to say something, but he threw me a sharp gaze and I closed it again.

"The school is going to try to expel you—you know that, don't you? They might even bring you up on charges."

Although I hadn't wanted to think about it, yes, I knew.

"I want you to tell me what evidence they have that it was you."

I considered the question carefully. "Nothing, really. I mean, there was this button from my shirt on Alec's driveway, but I didn't put it—"

"Circumstantial," he said. "Is that all?"

"That, and the fact that I knew about the penicillin."

He weighed the thought. "Well, then, they don't have much of a case."

There was something off about this—something not just in the tone of his voice, but the pattern of his thoughts.

"If there are any witnesses," he said, "it will be your word against theirs."

The heater in the car was on full blast, but I shivered all the same. *He thinks I did it.* It wasn't just Greene, or the other kids at school. My father thought that I was the kind of kid who would spike an allergic kid's chili with penicillin. Tears welled up in my eyes. I didn't even think about holding them back, but I did turn away from him, for fear that he'd think they were tears of guilt.

"There are lawyers who specialize in this sort of thing," he went on. "They can't expel you—you're innocent until proven guilty, no matter what you've done."

"No matter what I've done?" I turned to him, my vision mercifully blurred, so I didn't have to see the way he looked at me. "Dad, how can you talk like this?"

Then his jaw hardened, and I could sense that rage inside him again, but also an intense sadness. Tears being contagious in my family, his eyes began to fill. "We're talking about your future here, Jared. We're talking about your life. You want to save it, you tell them you're innocent, and you stick to it like glue to the very end."

"But I *am* innocent."

He took a long look at me then. So long that I had to remind him to look back at the road. He hit the brakes, and his trusty antilock brake system ground us to a halt halfway through an empty intersection. He backed up and waited for the light to change.

"I didn't do any of those things," I said, trying so hard to be sincere, it sounded like a lie. "You know that, Dad, don't you? . . . Don't you?"

He sighed and nodded reluctantly. I couldn't tell whether he believed me, or whether he was just showing his approval for an earnest lie.

"Well," he said, "all the more reason to tough it out."

If anyone could sleep after a drive like that, he's a better man than me. I lay awake that night, my head caught in endless loops of conversations that I'd never have. All the things I could have said to my father that would have convinced him I was telling the truth. All the things I could say to Alec, to make him turn his investigation—and his hatred elsewhere. Then I started thinking about what would happen if Alec's allergic reaction was much worse than anyone thought. What if he didn't make it? What if he died because some stupid idiot poisoned his chili, and what if the whole world was convinced it was me? That's the type of thing they put on the news. The type of thing they put on the cover of a hundred magazines to show how very screwed up some kids are, and isn't it terrible, and isn't it all because of TV and movies and Barney the dinosaur, and parents who sell insurance. And then they turn off their TVs, and throw away the magazine, and go on with their lives, thinking everything is so simple. Except it's not. Because if your own parents can't see into your head and know that there's someone in there who might not be all that innocent, but at least is innocent most of the time . . . if my own parents can't see what's always been good in me, then nothing can ever be simple again.

Fire
With Fire

ALEC DIDN'T DIE that day. In fact, he didn't even have to spend the night at the hospital. They pumped his stomach, shot him up with adrenaline, and gave him a Benadryl IV. He was home before dark.

Regardless of Alec's recovery, it was like a funeral when my parents drove me to school the next day for their meeting with the principal. Valentine's Day. Not much love went around today—in fact, my father said only one thing to me that morning. When I came out of my room, he took one look at me and said, "Change your clothes."

I looked at myself, realizing I was wearing my "bad" clothes. I had put them on without thinking. I changed silently into slacks and a plain shirt. One that had no missing buttons.

When we arrived, we suffered the indignation of sitting in the main office, in full view of everyone who passed by, until finally, ten minutes into first period, Principal Diller called us in. Only he didn't call all of us in. He had my parents go into his office. Me, he sent down the hall, to see Mr. Greene. Divide and conquer. I had learned about it in social studies.

A student escorted me to Mr. Greene's office. I recognized her as the girl from the chess team. The one who suggested that I teach Alec a lesson.

"For what it's worth, I think it was an excellent trick," she said to me.

I felt like lifting her up by her pigtails and screaming into her face. Instead I just said, "What if he died?"

She shook her head. "People don't die from allergic reactions. I'm allergic to cats, and it never killed me."

"Ever swallow a cat?" I asked. "Try it sometime, and we'll see if the allergic reaction kills you."

Mr. Greene was pacing outside of his office, waiting for me. Those last steps up to him felt like the thirteen steps up to the gallows, and no amount of denials would get me out of this.

"Good morning, Jared," Greene said as I approached him there in the hallway. "I suppose you know why you are here?"

There was no smug cockiness in his tone. Instead it was dead serious, and that was scary.

"How's Alec?" I asked.

"He's home today. We hope he'll be back by Friday." I took a deep, much needed breath of relief. "Understandably," said Mr. Greene, "his parents want to bring whoever did this up on criminal charges."

And one last time I looked Greene straight in the face. No attitude, no defenses, just the honest truth.

"I didn't do this, Mr. Greene."

And Mr. Greene said, "I know you didn't, Jared." Then he swung open the door to his office to reveal it was already full of people. Faces I knew—the Shadow Club.

I stepped in, wondering at first if I was the victim of some practical joke myself. The looks on everyone's faces made it clear that I wasn't. They were as scared, and worried as I was. Darren, Jason, O. P.—all of them, even Cheryl.

"They all came to my office right after school yesterday," Mr. Greene explained, "O. P. showed me this." He pulled from his desk the medical form O. P. had shown me, with the note on the back. **"We're on your side."**

"I told him why you were wearing that hat," Darren said. "Why you've been dressing that way. Going undercover and all."

"I told him exactly what happened at that meeting," said Jason.

"I didn't believe them at first," said Greene.

"Yeah," said Randall, "he thought it was some trick the Shadow Club had worked out to get ourselves off the hook."

"So what changed your mind?" I asked.

"I did," said a voice that I wasn't expecting to hear. As I moved deeper into the office, I saw that someone was sitting in the Electric Chair. Not a member of the Shadow Club, not even close—it was Austin Pace.

"Why don't the rest of you get back to class," Mr. Greene said.

The Shadow Club filed out and left me alone with Austin and Mr. Greene.

"It was you, Austin?" I said incredulously. "You pulled all those pranks? You poisoned Alec's lunch?"

Mr. Greene answered for him.

"No," Mr. Greene said, "but what he did wasn't much better."

Austin wouldn't look at me. Mr. Greene had to prompt him. "Why don't you tell him, Austin."

I sat down in one of the softer chairs reserved for kids who needed kindness instead of discipline.

"I put your button on Alec's driveway."

"What?!"

"I didn't think anyone would actually find it," said Austin, already getting defensive.

"But . . . but how did you get ahold of my button?"

"Dinner at my house, remember?" Austin said. "You lost it then."

"There's more," Mr. Greene said. "Go on, Austin." Austin threw me a quick glance, then looked down.

"I heard some noises outside the night that it happened. Alec lives across the street from me, and I looked out of my bedroom window that night. I saw somebody running away. I couldn't tell who it was, but I knew it wasn't you, because, believe me, I know the way you run, Jared."

He tried to say something else, but it seemed hard in coming. He looked at Mr. Greene, he looked at me, then he looked at his own fidgeting hands. "But even if I hadn't seen it, I would have known it wasn't you, because I knew you wouldn't do something like that again—not after what happened to me."

More than anything else, hearing that from Austin was like a pardon from prison. It suddenly struck me how strange it was that of all the people in school, the one who knew me well enough to know that my heart really was in the right place was my old adversary, Austin Pace.

"Why, Austin?" I asked. "If you knew it wasn't me, then why did you put the button there?"

Then he looked at me, his face twisted in conflicting emotions: guilt, anger, frustration.

"Because I wanted it to be you."

Mr. Greene dismissed Austin, who was happy to get out of there as quickly as possible. Then Mr. Greene sat on the edge of his desk and said, "I owe you an apology, Jared. For the way I've been treating you, for not believing you, for thinking the worst. For all that, I'm sorry."

They were words I thought I would never hear Mr. Greene utter. I had to admit I had him pegged, too, as the type of guy who would weasel out of an apology, even when he knew he was dead wrong. I guess we both had misjudged each other, because it took a lot of guts for someone like him to apologize to a fourteen-year-old kid.

"And my parents?"

"Principal Diller is letting them know that you're off the hook. He doesn't know the details yet, but we'll go down there in a bit to fill them all in."

"Good," I said. "Maybe you can apologize to them, too."

Mr. Greene grinned at that. "Fair enough. I owe you that."

I could literally feel the weight being lifted off my shoulders. My chest didn't feel so tight, and although my legs were sore from all the running I did yesterday, I felt like I could jump up and touch the ceiling. I could have just accepted that sense of vindication and left, but quitting while I was ahead was never one of my strong points.

"There's just one problem," I said. "We still don't know who's been pulling all these pranks."

"It's not your problem anymore," Mr. Greene said.

"Even so," I told him, "I'd like to finish what I've started, and flush out the creep."

Mr. Greene crossed his arms, looking at me no longer as a subject to study and dissect, but more like an equal—someone who had earned his respect. I never thought I would care about that.

"What do you have in mind?" he asked.

It was a fantastic plan if I do say so myself. Everyone would have to work together to pull off the scam of the century—

or at least the school year. It would take me, the members of the Shadow Club. It would take Principal Diller and school security, but it would also take Alec. He had the most crucial role to play. Although Alec hated me, I knew once Principal Diller sat him down and talked to him, he would play his part, because it would make him look real good.

I didn't see him, or speak to him about it, but Mr. Greene assured me that Principal Diller was taking care of it, and he'd be much more responsive to the principal than to me.

On Thursday night I wasn't good for much of anything. I was nervous, like an actor before the opening of a play. I sat at my desk staring at that blue denim cap with TSC in bright orange letters across the face.

Tyson came in, and I tried to hide the cap, but I was way too conspicuous about it. I wanted to tell him about our plan to flush out the rat in our school but somehow felt it would be wrong. He didn't need any more complications in his life.

"That's Jodi Lattimer's hat, isn't it?" he said.

I shrugged. "Tennis and Squash Center," I said. "Actually, lots of kids are wearing them now."

"But *that* one's Jodi's," he said.

"How can you tell?"

"The way the brim is curled. I notice things like that." He started to leave, probably assuming that Jodi and I had something between us. I stopped him.

"It's not what you think," I said.

"Who said I think anything?"

He went back to his room and closed the door. Not with a slam, but hard enough to mean business. I wondered if the morning would bring more of his fire sketches.

Alec was back in school on Friday, in time for the candidate debates. The day off had done wonders for him. There was no sign that he had had the allergic reaction at all. He and his parents supposedly were told by Principal Diller himself that I was not responsible for what happened, but Alec still avoided me that day. He wouldn't even make eye contact with me, and that was fine by me, because I wasn't quite ready to talk to him either.

The candidate debates went on as scheduled. Tommy Nickols tried to change his campaign slogan to "The thinking *person's* candidate," but no spin doctor could patch up his earlier image. The final blow came when his girlfriend tried to dump him. Apparently she was more important than his quest for power, and he quit, putting his backing behind Katrina Mendelson. Alec's video ploy had rattled some votes away from Cheryl, according to the school poll, and since Katrina Mendelson was giving free, home-baked cookies to anyone who promised to vote for her, she was picking up steam. Still, Alec was way out in the lead. Although half the school couldn't stomach seeing him succeed again, the other half was ready to follow him into victory. And now the sympathy vote, which often went to Katrina in the past, was going to him, because he was the only candidate who had been glued, skunked, hair-balled, and poisoned.

By the time I arrived at school that day, everything was in place for the big show. Not the debate, but *my* big show. Although I was nervous, I knew I wasn't alone—each member of the Shadow Club was behind me, and so was Mr. Greene—even Principal Diller had a role to play. When I walked into the auditorium, the Shaditude had grown around me. It was no longer just an aura, it moved before me like a compression wave, and I rode the wave for the first time, allowing myself to really enjoy it, knowing it would be the last time I would feel the sense of head-turning power, even if it was just illusion. I could make a very successful creep, I thought, and although that should have bothered me, somehow it didn't. Perhaps because I knew I never would want to be one.

The debate questions were posed by people in the audience—people handpicked by their teachers, of course. I waited, not even hearing the questions or answers, just generating the nerve to do what I was there to do. I do remember one question, though. *What qualities make you the best candidate for the job?* Alec was asked. His answer was, *Because I'm not afraid to fight injustice, and I can tell the truth no matter how well the lies are concealed.* His words were directed at me, with that same cold stare he gave me before he knew I wasn't the one tormenting him. But I didn't have time to think about what was going on in Alec's head. I just assumed he was playing his part in the show, and I took it as my cue to stand. Principal Diller, the moderator, acknowledged me, and I came to the microphone to ask my question, feeling that compression wave of the Shaditude pushing around me, bringing me a chorus of whispers, then silencing the auditorium as I approached. It was so quiet you could hear the steam gently hissing through the radiator coils.

"I want to know," I said into the microphone, my voice larger than life, "I want to know how Alec can stand up there and say he has any self-respect whatsoever after I so completely humiliated him." The gasps and murmurs around the room rose in a wave, then silence fell again.

"Mr. Mercer," said Principal Diller, "exactly what are you saying?"

"You know what I'm saying," I answered. "How does it feel, Alec," I said, "to stand up there knowing that I'm out here, the one who glued your hands to your head, the one who skunked you, the one who gave you some chili-cillin and put a clump of my own hair in your soda? How does it feel to look at me and know that you can't do anything about it?"

I could see his face going red and was impressed by his acting ability—he was really playing this one for all that it was worth.

"There's something I can do about it, all right."

"I admit it," I said. "I did all those things. Me and the Shadow Club. So what are you going to do about it?"

"If you want to see the type of guy who'll lead you into the upper grades," he told the audience, "then watch me now."

By now Mr. Greene was heading toward me from the back of the auditorium with a security guard.

"Mr. Diller, it's time that the Shadow Club pays for what it's done. Their time is up." Mr. Diller came out from behind the moderator's podium. Slowly the growing murmur of the crowd became a roar. I felt as though I was in the middle of a courtroom and not a junior high school debate. I half expected Principal Diller to bang a gavel and tell everyone to come to order. Instead he said, "Mr. Greene, will you have Jared Mercer escorted out, along with all the other members of the Shadow Club."

The other members were in the audience as well, spread out in various locations, each of them wearing Tennis and Squash Center hats. It had been easy to get a hat for everyone—there were enough of them around school. It was just a matter of buying or borrowing them from other kids. Even Cheryl as she stood there behind her debate podium pulled out a TSC hat and proudly put it on, to the stunned amazement of everyone gathered. The result was perfect. We had everyone fooled! That's when the security guard, who was in on it, too, took handcuffs out from his back pocket and cuffed me.

"We have zero tolerance for the Shadow Club," Mr. Diller said. "Or for any gang, now or ever. All members of the Shadow Club are expelled from this school, effective immediately." And every last one of us was escorted out, with me in the lead with my hands cuffed behind my back. It was so realistic that for a few moments even I was scared as we walked down the hallway toward the main office.

"Okay," I said to the security guard, who was holding my arm a little too tightly, "you can take these off now."

"I don't think so," he said.

I looked at him in shock, and he looked at me with those hard dark eyes of his.

Then he cracked a smile. "Hah!" he said. "You should have seen the look on your face!"

"Very funny."

We were escorted into the teachers' lounge. Mr. Greene showed up a few minutes later after the bell had rung and kids were passing. The smoked glass on the teachers'-lounge door made it impossible for other kids to see all seven of us relaxing on the sofa, munching on chips, and enjoying the guilty pleasure of being in one of the few places that is completely off-limits to students.

"That was one heck of an act," Mr. Greene said. "You had me believing it."

"So what happens now?" asked Darren. "Now that we are EXPELLED." He laughed at the word.

"We wait," I told them.

"For what?" asked Jason.

"For someone to crack—right, Mr. Greene?"

Mr. Greene nodded. "The person who did this will crack one way or another. Either by cracking under the guilt at having gotten you all expelled or by bragging to friends, frustrated that you got all the credit."

I took off my TSC hat and looked at it, laughing.

"These things sure came in handy, didn't they?"

"Yeah," said Abbie. "Good thing for the Tennis and Squash Center."

And that's when Principal Diller stuck a pin in our swelled little balloon of a plan.

"What Tennis and Squash Center?" he asked.

"You know, *the* Tennis and Squash Center."

Principal Diller laughed. "I play squash—there's no Tennis and Squash Center in town. We've been trying to get one for years, but the nearest courts are twenty miles away."

The room fell silent, and I felt the way Alec must have felt when he peered into that cup and saw the hair ball. "Then . . . what does TSC stand for?" I kept looking at my hat, like it might answer me, then it finally began to dawn on me how wrong we'd been—all of us—about so many things. "Oh no . . ."

"How many of these hats have you seen around school?" Greene asked.

"I don't know," said Cheryl. "Ten . . . maybe twenty . . . maybe more."

And for one absurd little instant, a cartoon image of Mickey Mouse came to me. I saw him hacking apart an enchanted broom, only to find that when he wasn't looking, each splinter had grown arms and a will of its own. But instead of buckets in their hands, each of ours wore a hat on its head with the unmistakable insignia of "The Shadow Club."

Weekend Warriors

WHEN A STORM system is about to move through town, you can usually tell it's coming. The wind picks up, and the ocean starts churning. A storm came to town that long Presidents' Day weekend, but it didn't come by way of land or sea. It came by foot.

It began with Solerno's. Patrons sat there at lunchtime on Saturday, hoping against hope that their pizza might have a little less salt and garlic, when someone found something crunchy underneath the cheese. The story, which rumbled through town like thunder, hit me after who knows how many ears. Cheryl told me about it. "It wasn't exactly a sausage in the pizza," she said, "but you can say it was full of protein."

It was, in fact, a cockroach. Industrial-sized. As the story goes, Solerno then opened his storeroom to find everything from the flour to the Parmesan cheese infested with hundreds upon hundreds of roaches. It was too late to stop some of them from being baked into the pizza and lasagna. Although I can't be sure, I had a sneaking suspicion that one or more of his various part-time pizza makers wore a TSC hat.

I know tales get exaggerated in the telling, but I believe the part about Old Man Solerno bursting into tears, and swearing he'd never open his doors again.

Victim number two: Mrs. Hilda McBroom. More commonly known, even to our parents, as Broom Hilda, the Witch. Widowed since before I was born, it seemed her one remaining goal in life was to keep kids from getting anywhere near her beautiful rose garden. In the spring and summer, that garden was beautiful indeed. Her yard was full of trellises that sprouted roses in every color of the spectrum. She had recently cut them back in preparation for the growing season, but on this particular Sunday, she awoke to find that her rosebushes had been cut back a bit further. Like all the way to the roots. Every single rosebush had been beheaded like Marie Antoinette, never again to sprout another rose. Rumor was that she just stood outside in the middle of the thorny debris for an hour, until a neighbor led her back into her house.

Victim number three: Garson Underwood, a computer programmer who seemed to have been targeted for no other reason than the fact that he was amazingly fat. Me, I never had a problem with fat people unless they sat next to me on an airplane—but then, it's not their fault that airplane seats are so small—and it's not Garson's fault that his own body decided to be his enemy, refusing to burn off his fat. I knew he tried to slim down, because I often saw him running desperately. Anyway, Garson emerged from his house that Sunday morning to find his car had been spammed. I mean completely—there had to have been a dozen industrial-sized cans of Spam spread over every inch of his brand-new Caddy—but that was only the icing on the cake. After he cleaned off the Spam, and he tried to start the engine, it kept coughing and dying. What he didn't know was that the gas tank had been filled to the brim with molten Ben & Jerry's Chunky Monkey ice cream, the radiator was loaded with Mountain Dew, and several pounds of butter had been spread over the engine block.

After several attempts to start the engine, the spark plugs set the butter on fire, the car was soon engulfed in flames, and Mr. Underwood could do nothing but watch from the sidewalk as his new Cadillac went up in flames.

Victim number four: Ms. Regina Pfeiffer, children's librarian at our public library. She had become a friend of mine a few years back when she taught me, much to my surpirse, that there were tons of books I'd actually enjoy—even ones by dead writers. The attack on her began with a broken window in the library on Saturday night. In the morning the police found that almost all the books were gone from the kids' section. The only one left, right on a middle shelf, was *The Chocolate War*, which made sickeningly perfect sense, since the rest of the library was doused in Hershey's syrup. As for all the other books, they came washing up on the beach that day, the way jellyfish did in the summer.

More tales drifted in all weekend long, and what made it more frightening was that these stories all made the rounds by Sunday afternoon, which meant the culprits were actually bragging about what they had done. They couldn't wait for the stories to work their way down the grapevine.

Cheryl and I tried to track down the originators of the stories, knowing that the first person to tell the tale was probably involved in the crime, but by now everyone was suspect. Everyone *except* the original members of the Shadow Club.

We had gathered at Cheryl's house, and each member of the club was assigned the task of tracking down the person who had given them their TSC hat.

"What do we do when we find them?" O. P. asked. "Make a citizen's arrest?"

Jason chuckled nervously. "You want me to try to arrest Arliss Booth? He's not called the 'Pile Driver' for nothing. Even the football team's afraid of him."

"Besides, it's not like we have any proof," Abbie said.

"All we need is one confession," I told them.

"Yeah, right," said Randall. "They're just gonna swing open their door and spill their guts to us."

"Maybe so. Somebody's got to be feeling guilty."

"Don't be so sure," said Darren. "The more kids involved, the less guilty each one feels. We all know about that, don't we?"

Yes, we did know, and it made the situation that much graver. They left, leaving Cheryl and me alone.

"Do you remember who else was wearing those hats?" Cheryl asked.

I shook my head. I remembered the hats, but not a single face beneath them. "I'd better just start with Jodi."

"Do you know where she lives?"

"No, but I can find out."

Cheryl paused for a second. "Maybe you should ask Tyson. He'll know."

"I don't like the idea of bringing this up to Tyson. He'll think I'm accusing him."

"What if he's involved?"

"No—he's not violent like that."

"You don't call setting fires violent?"

"Yeah, but it was always a reaction to something someone else had done to him. It's like he's allergic to abuse from other kids and has a violent reaction to it. He wouldn't just go out and trash people's lives."

"But his girlfriend would."

"So did mine." It came out before I had the chance to hold back. Cheryl reeled as if I had slugged her in the face. "I'm sorry I said that."

"No," she said. "Never be sorry for telling the truth."

The next few moments were awkward and uncertain. Cheryl and I had never discussed Austin's broken ankle and the rocks she had spread out in the field. Although she made a full confession, I was the one who took the brunt of the blame. I didn't realize how much I had resented that, until now.

"I'm sorry about what happened to Austin," she said. "I still can't believe I could do something so horrible."

I took her hand and gently squeezed it. "You're not doing anything horrible now. But there are others who are."

She nodded, then she slipped her hand out from mine, and we got back to work.

"Did you hear about what happened down at the Gazilliaplex?" Jodi asked me when she answered her door not half an hour later. The Gazilliaplex was our local movie theater. It claimed the capacity to show more movies than were actually in release on any given day, but they usually just showed four or five movies on a gazillion different screens.

"When they opened today," she continued, "they found cows in the projection rooms chewing up the film and smashing all the equipment. Weird, huh?" Well, maybe not so weird, considering the fact that the owner of the Gazilliaplex was hated by kids because he ejected anyone who got caught trying to theater-surf and was fond of calling the people waiting in line "cattle."

"Tell me, Jodi, how could you know what happened when the theater only opened fifteen minutes ago?"

"Well, I just heard."

I paced a little bit on her porch, a bit unnerved by how calm she was.

"So why are you here?" she asked. "It's not like you can ask me to the movies now." She giggled. "Not unless they're showing *Steer Wars*."

I turned to her sharply. "I want names," I demanded. "I want to know who it is—every last one of them, and how many there are."

She twisted her lip in a disgusted snarl. "I don't know what you're talking about."

"Yeah, sure you don't. You're just as innocent as can be."

"You're acting too weird, Jared." The honesty in her expression was the most unnerving thing of all. How could she lie and lie and still not show it in her eyes? As for me, I couldn't imagine what my eyes must have been like by now.

"You're involved, and we both know it."

"I'm not involved in anything. I was at a sleepover with my friends last night."

"Swear it," I blurted.

"I swear."

"Still not good enough."

"OK, I swear on my grandmother's grave."

"Not good enough."

"Do you want me to put my hand on a Bible?"

"Yes," I said. "Yes, I do."

And she said without any hesitation, "Fine, I'll go get one." But before she went inside, she thought for a moment, and said, "Just because there're some people in town who are finally getting what they deserve, that doesn't mean me, or any of my friends are involved." Then she added, "Nobody wanted to see you expelled, Jared, but when you think about it, isn't it more likely that you and *your* friends did it?"

That left me speechless. "But . . . but the hats."

"They're just hats," she said, shrugging the whole thing off. "What does a hat prove?" Then she smiled at me. "I'll go get that Bible."

She went inside, but I left before she came back, because I knew that no matter what she had done, she *would* put her hand on that Bible, look me in the eye, and swear.

I went home after that. My mind was trying to roll into self-preservation mode by now, trying to convince me of all the things I'd rather be doing. Watching videos, playing computer games, net surfing, I'd even be happy to do homework now. But when I got home I couldn't bring myself to do much of anything at all. Tyson was gone, my parents were out, and I found myself just staring at the blinking light on the answering machine. I didn't want to hear any more bad news, so I just sat there, tossing that seashell of mine up and down, putting it to my ear, wishing I could hear a voice in there that might magically solve all my problems.

Finally I went to the answering machine and hit the button.

"Hi, Jared . . . this is Darren." I took a deep breath. Of all the ex-members of the Shadow Club, I figured Darren would be the least likely to call me. His voice sounded shaky. Scared. I hit the pause button, took a few deep breaths, then let the message continue.

"You gotta get down here," he said "It's Mr. Greene. See, I live on his block and . . . well . . . just get down here." And the message ended.

I left the house and made the long run alone to find out what had happened to Mr. Greene.

IF THE OTHER things had been mean-spirited, what they did to Mr. Greene was downright evil. Darren was nowhere to be found when I got to his house. The curtains were drawn; no one answered the door. Clearly the only part he wanted in this was to be the messenger. He expected me to be the one to do something about it. Giving up on Darren, I made my way down the street toward Mr. Greene's home.

Sometimes houses are eerie. Their windows can be eyes, their door a mouth. Today Mr. Greene's house didn't just resemble a face; it looked like a corpse. The police had already come and gone, leaving behind the paint-splattered house, with broken windows. When I saw it I wanted to leave, but I knew I couldn't. I knew I had to go in there and see it for myself. Not the way you have to see an accident by the side of the road, but the way you sometimes have to sift through the wreckage of a storm to see if some part of your own life is lying there, too.

He was inside, slowly picking through the wreckage.

There was a lot of it. Anything breakable was broken, and the things that would not break had heavy dents that could only have come from a baseball bat.

Mr. Greene was being careful with the debris, gingerly picking up pieces of a broken plate, as though it still could be used, carefully placing it into a plastic trash bag. His motions were deliberate, respectful. He was so wrapped up in the task, he didn't notice me there.

"This looks worse than my room," I said.

He turned toward me, but didn't appear to be surprised to see me.

"And you thought you had no friends."

"What do you mean?"

Mr. Greene shook his head bitterly. "Don't you see? This was retaliation. Your plan worked, Jared; we convinced the whole school that you and the Shadow Club were expelled. So your secret admirers decided to retaliate."

Until that moment it hadn't occurred to me that any of this had been done for my benefit—as if it were something I wanted.

He returned to his task. Now he was trying to piece together the shredded fragments of a canvas. The empty frame lay in pieces on the exposed springs of an easy chair that wasn't so easy anymore.

I knelt down to help, as if anything we did could actually fix the painting.

"It's an original Thomas Kinkaid," he said. "We had always talked about getting one. My wife got it for our anniversary one year."

"I didn't know you were married."

"Was. My wife died some time ago."

I looked down. "I'm sorry."

But he just waved it off. "It was a long time ago—before I even moved here."

It's funny, but I never imagined my teachers having a life outside of school. I mean, sure I know that they did—but knowing and being able to imagine that life were two different things. I couldn't picture Mr. Greene doing anything but trying to get inside kids' heads to figure what made them tick. Knowing he had a past was an unexpected challenge to what Mr. Greene would call my "comfort zone."

I pieced two of the colorful strips close together and blurred my vision to make the rip go away, but that illusion didn't last long.

"I'm sure whoever did this didn't know," I said.

Mr. Greene only scoffed. "Do you think it would have stopped them if they *did* know?"

Mr. Greene took one more look at the fragmented landscape, and sighed. "What turns kids into monsters, Jared?" It was a strange thing to hear from a guidance counselor.

"Is this a multiple choice or an essay question?" I responded, holding up a strip of the torn canvas. "Because if it's an essay, I'm gonna need more paper."

He actually laughed at that. Not much of one, but at least it was something.

"I don't know," I said. "Maybe some kids are born that way." But even as I said it, I knew it wasn't that easy—because *I* had been a monster for a while. I wasn't born that way. I didn't stay that way either. So maybe I didn't know where the monsters came from, but I think I did know how to get rid of them.

"Silver bullets," I said before I even knew what I meant.

"Excuse me."

"You need a silver bullet to get rid of a monster. That, or a stake through the heart."

"Is this a joke?"

"No . . . What I mean is that it takes something really sharp and painful to kill that monster once it shows up in a kid—otherwise the monster will keep on going."

Mr. Greene nodded, realizing what I was saying. "Painful like almost drowning Tyson?" he reminded. "Like driving him to burn down his own home?"

I grimaced at the thought, and mimed pulling a stake out of my heart. "Yeah." Watching Tyson's house burn down was like receiving a silver bullet and stake at the same time. Living through that was more than enough to kill my nasty little monster.

Mr. Greene looked at me then in that vice-principalish sort of way. "One problem with your silver bullet theory," he said. "When Tyson almost died, it truly was your silver bullet. But this time, none of it stopped when Alec almost died. It only got worse." He didn't have to say anymore for me to know what he meant, and it was too awful to say aloud—as if mentioning it would make it so.

If this new armor-plated Shadow Club was resistant to silver bullets, it would take a mightier blow to kill it and make these kids see reason. Yes, someone had almost died, but for this new improved Shadow Club, almost wasn't good enough.

I didn't go home after that—Tyson might be back, and I couldn't face him. Did he have any clue that his girlfriend was a monster? Did it ever cross his mind that the girl of his dreams was at the heart of everyone else's nightmare, along with who knew how many others? I wanted to tell my parents, and have Jodi brought to justice, but my imagination began to twist all my thoughts. What if my parents didn't believe me? What if Jodi and her conspirators told better lies than I told the truth? I was the one acting shifty, not her. Who would *anyone* believe? Sure, my parents had been set straight by Principal Diller, but that didn't matter. They had been convinced I was capable of pure premeditated evil. That was different from what happened back in October. Back then, the evil snuck up on me—I never knew it was there until it ran its course and did all its damage. But I knew better now. To know better but to still follow that path would put me in a different class completely—a path my parents had believed I had chosen.

With so much hanging over my head at home, I decided to go to Cheryl's instead. I'm sure she had heard even more stories of cruelty racing through the well-worn gossip lines. She would be feeling much the same way I was. They say misery loves company, but I don't think that's true. I wasn't looking forward to sharing Mr. Greene's plight with Cheryl, I just felt I had no other choice.

I fought my instinct to run to her house. I was always running. Mostly I just ran in circles, but lately my pace had become erratic, my goal uncertain. I was no longer running a circuit, but a maze. So today I walked, forcing my feet to conform to the slower pace.

All the way to Cheryl's house, I kept having the uncanny feeling I was being watched. Paranoia, I told myself. So much unwanted attention had been thrown in my direction lately that I figured it was just my mind playing tricks on me. If I had listened to my intuition then, things might have come out a lot differently. I'm still not sure if that's good or bad. But the way it happened, I never saw it coming. I never felt the blow to my head before it was lights out.

There are a lot of things about being knocked unconscious that you can only learn from experience. Like that strange sense of disorientation when you come to, and losing the memory of how and where you got knocked out to begin with. That's how it was with me, when I woke up in a swiveling bucket seat in a van that stunk to high heaven.

"Welcome back, loser," said a voice that I only dimly recognized. "How was dreamland?"

I tried to move my arms and legs but couldn't. At first I thought it was me—that I had somehow been paralyzed— but then I realized my arms and legs were tied to the plush leather seat by safety belts that had been cut from the van. It was hard enough to get out of those things when they were just tangled—but tied, there was no hope of freeing myself.

My mouth tasted like blood, and the putrid smell in the air made me want to gag. It smelled of disinfectant and air freshener, but underneath it all was the unyielding stench of skunk. I thought it was dark outside, but then I realized the van was in a garage—Alec's *detached* garage, far enough from his house so even if I screamed no one would hear me.

"I gave you the best seat," Alec said. "The one that swivels." He kicked my seat, turning me sharply around to face him. He sat in the bench seat in the back. The moment I saw his eyes I knew something was horribly wrong.

"Of course, that's also the seat that the skunk sprayed, but only the best for Jared Mercer."

"Alec—what are you, nuts? What am I doing here? ~~h~~at do you want?"

He didn't answer. He only smiled, but it was more like a grimace. A leer. Suddenly I felt like I was being crushed under the wheels of the van rather than sitting in it.

"The school might think expelling you was punishment enough, but it's not enough for me," Alec said, kicking my chair again. I spun around and around until he caught the chair with his foot.

"Expelled? What are you talking about?" But one more look at his face and I knew. The pain throbbing in my head now beat a faster, heavier rhythm. "Principal Diller never told you?"

"Never told me what?" The contempt in his voice was proof of how bad the break in communication had been. It all made sense now—how well Alec had played his part during the debate, how his voice had quivered with anger, how his face had turned red. He hadn't been acting! He had thought it was real! It was widely known, even among the students, that Principal "Diller Do-Wrong" was an occasional screwup. But he never screwed up when it really mattered. Until now.

"It was all an act," I tried to explain. "It was an act to flush out the person who *really* did all those things to you! You were supposed to know. *How could you not know?*"

"You'd lie to get out of anything, wouldn't you? You're so pathetic."

I was light-years away from reaching him—he was so far

gone in his hatred and need for revenge that nothing I could say would convince him. I was scared now. As scared as I was in that burning lighthouse, because I knew that Alec was tipping over the edge.

"Alec," I said calmly, burying my fear as deep inside as I could, "you have to let me go. This is a misunderstanding. Whatever you're going to do, you'll be sorry you did it. So untie me, and let's just walk out of here."

"Forget it." He hopped up and grabbed something behind the seat. Something big. It was, of all things, a big empty water jug—a clear plastic twenty-gallon bottle, the kind they use for watercoolers. We used to use those things to bat tennis balls—grip the neck, swing away, and tennis balls would fly for a mile. But the neck had been sawed off this water jug, and the hole was covered with duct tape.

"How about a taste of your own medicine?" Alec held up the jug so I could see inside. Few things in the world could have frightened me more than I already was—but what I saw in that jug brought me to a new level of despair.

The jug was full of bees.

"How allergic are you to these things, Jared?" he asked cheerfully.

"A single sting . . . could kill me." I tried to show him my med-alert bracelet, but as usual I wasn't wearing it.

"A single sting, huh? What happens? Does your head swell up like a balloon and pop? Does your tongue turn purple and your eyes explode?"

I swallowed hard. "Something like that." Everything I said just goaded him further. He was loving this, and he didn't care. At this moment he didn't care how sorry he'd feel tomorrow, and by then it wouldn't matter to me either, because I'd be dead.

"Please, Alec," I begged. "Please, I'll do anything. ANY-THING you want. I'll leave town. I'll run away. You'll never have to see me again—just *please don't let the bees loose*."

"I wasn't planning to let the bees loose."

I breathed a shuddering sigh of relief, until he said, "If I let them loose, they might sting me, too." Then he pulled a single strip of duct tape from the opening, leaving a slit about eight inches long. "These bees are just for you." He lifted the jug in both hands, turned it upside down, and in a single swift motion, jammed it down over my head.

Instantly I was on the inside. A dozen bees swarmed around my head, bumping into my cheek, my neck, my eyebrows, as lethal as bullets. I wanted to scream but couldn't. I didn't dare open my mouth, because they'd fly inside and sting my throat. I would suffocate on my own swollen tonsils. I tugged my hands, but the bonds wouldn't give. I rolled my shoulders, but still the jug wouldn't come off. It just tilted left and right, forward and backward.

I could see Alec now through the plastic, as though I was looking out from a fishbowl. He wasn't laughing or even grinning anymore. The look on his face almost mirrored my own, but he was unable to stop himself.

A bee had rested on the rim of my ear. I could feel it spiral around until it was forcing itself into my ear canal, probing deeper as if my ear were the mouth of a flower. Finally I came to my own edge, and felt myself slipping off.

I screamed. I didn't care if the bees got in my mouth now, I didn't care about anything. All I cared about was the sound of my scream, echoing in the jug.

I barely noticed the light suddenly pouring into the garage, or the sliding door of the van opening. I barely saw Alec being pulled out, and when the jug was finally pulled off my head and I saw Jodi—wonderful, horrible Jodi—standing there, with Tyson right beside her, I still screamed. Even after the jug was gone, I still kept on screaming, believing, in my heart of hearts, that I would never stop.

Because of Alec.

Because of the bees.

And because Tyson was wearing a hat that said TSC.

Oxy-morons

ALEC HAD DISAPPEARED by the time Jodi and Tyson untied me, pulled away by kids whose faces I didn't see. "They're giving Alec what he deserves," Jodi said.

As soon as my arms were free, I felt all over my face and neck, still expecting the telltale swelling that would come from a lethal bee sting—but I had been lucky. Now the intense fear I had felt resolved into an aching head, and a weary sense of mental vagueness, like I was watching all this from a distance. Or maybe I just wished I was.

I followed them from Alec's house, downhill, wishing I could go home, but not feeling strong enough to do anything but follow.

"I'm really not a part of it," Tyson said on the way, when Jodi had gotten a few paces ahead and couldn't hear. "You've got to believe me."

"I believe you."

"I haven't done a thing, you've got to believe me."

"I believe you."

"She just told me today—I wouldn't be caught dead wearing this hat if Jodi and I weren't going out, you have to believe that."

"I believe it." But apparently Tyson had a harder time convincing himself than he did convincing me.

"Where did they take Alec?" I asked Jodi.

"Where do you think?" she said.

I followed them to the Ghosties, and to the tugboat, still resting in its cradle at the edge of the seawall. I climbed up through the hole in the hull to find them all there, crowding the hull of the old boat. Not seven or eight kids. Not a dozen, but thirty, maybe more. Kids from younger grades, maybe even a high schooler or two, all of them proudly wearing that terrible hat. It was late in the day now, and the weird upside-down attic space was lit by at least a dozen flashlights aimed at odd angles, casting jagged shadows that made Frankensteins out of everyone's faces.

And they all came to me when they saw me.

"Hey, Jared," they said. "Good to see you." They put their hands up for high fives, and when I didn't return them, they just clapped me on my shoulder or back as I passed, heading toward the front of the boat where their new leader awaited. It was Brett Whatley.

"I knew you'd end up with us sooner or later," said Brett, his arms crossed proudly as he stood toward the front, straddling the V-shaped hull. Moose SanGiorgio was also there, lurking large in the shadows. As always, his hulking presence enhanced the bitter flavor of the situation. Behind Brett was a wooden post supporting the deck up above. Tied to that post was Alec, or what was left of him.

Whatever they had done to him, they had done it quickly. His clothes were covered in mud, or at least I hoped it was mud. His face was swollen, bruised, and bleeding.

I turned to Moose. "You were supposed to be his body-guards!"

Moose raised his eyebrows. "We were double agents."

"It was my idea," Brett had to add.

My head was still pounding, my ears still buzzed with the memory of the bees. All I wanted to do was crawl up into a ball in the corner and let all this be someone else's problem, but I couldn't. The sight of Alec, battered as he was, brought my senses back into focus, and my thoughts back into clarity.

"What makes you think Alec won't tell who did this to him?"

"He won't tell," said Jodi, "because he knows if he does, it will only get worse."

"Yeah," echoed Brett. "Alec has paid his debt to society. After today, if he doesn't bother us, we don't bother him."

But somehow I found that hard to believe.

"As you can see, this is bigger than you now, Jared," Brett said.

"No sense fighting it," added Jodi as she took her place

beside Brett. So they were the ringleaders now, like Cheryl and I had been, but while Cheryl and I were fueled by resentment, these two were fueled by hate. You could feel it radiating from them like an aura. You could smell it as strongly as skunk.

"Alec thought it was you doing all that stuff to him!" Brett laughed. "He didn't have a clue."

"It was my hair in his soda," said Jackson Belmont.

"But I put it in," said J. J. Welsh, who worked the fair's food concession.

"I gave them the skunk," Jodi said.

"But *we* put it in the minivan," said the Rangley twins.

"I had some fun with Lunar Glue," said Angela Wyndham.

"I had some leftover penicillin," Wendy Gorman said.

I looked around me. All of them were guilty. And they were proud of it.

Brett gloated. "We are your last best defense against the scum of the universe."

I shook my head. "Tommy Lee Jones—*Men in Black*. You still can't come up with an original line, Brett."

Brett just shrugged.

"Keep dealing in hatred," I said, "and it'll bite you in the ass."

Still nothing. "Our hatred is justified," he said.

Justified hatred? "Oxymoron." I said.

That got a reaction from Brett. "What did you call me?"

Jodi grabbed him before he could lunge at me. "It means two things that don't make sense together. Like 'jumbo shrimp.'"

But I was also thinking of it the other way, because all that hatred was definitely keeping this pack of morons from getting enough oxygen to the brain. Unfortunately they needed something more than just fresh air, but I didn't know what it was.

I turned to Tyson. "You're okay with all of this?"

If his shoulders sank any lower they'd be dragging on the floor. "Not exactly . . ."

I knew I should have been pissed at him, but I wasn't, because I knew who he was, and what he had come from. He had gone from being the neighborhood outcast, to being accepted, and even dating the girl of his dreams. Today he was being asked to sell his soul to keep his new station in life. I knew it was tearing him apart. Still, I noticed he had taken off his TSC hat.

I looked at Alec. I'm sure he heard all of this. Even with swollen eyes I could see him watching, but when I approached him he turned away, unable to look me in the face. I knew what he was feeling now—hatred for the others, and guilt for what he had done to me. It wasn't just his face that was screwed up, it was his soul now, because he had been at the edge. He had tried to kill me, and the memory would be with him all his life.

I went up to Alec. I don't know what I felt for him—disgust, pity, anger—but regardless of how I felt, I knew one thing was true, and I knew Alec needed to hear it.

"I forgive you," I told him. He turned his head away. But I grabbed his chin and forced him to look at me. "Listen to me, you lousy SOB! I understand why you did what you did to me. I forgive you." I let go of his face, and this time he kept eye contact with me.

"I'm sorry," he said weakly.

I nodded. "Apology accepted." Then I turned toward Brett, speaking loudly enough so that everyone could hear.

"This ends here."

"I don't think so," said Brett. He was in his element now, the power going straight to that slab of meat loaf he called a brain.

"There are an awful lot of people in this town who need to be taught a lesson," Jodi chimed in.

"We've got lists," added Moose.

"Yeah," said Brett. "Lots of them—and everyone on those lists is gonna get what's coming to them."

The chess girl came up behind me. "It's a good thing, Jared—you'll see."

"Yeah," added Tommy Nickols. "People around here will start thinking twice before doing things that bug us."

"Who made you judge and jury?" I asked them all.

"*You* did, Jared," answered Jodi. "The whole thing was your idea, remember? That's why we trashed Greene's place for you. That's why we saved you from Alec today. That's why we brought you here."

Hearing her say that heated my blood to a boil. I had done some awful things, but I would not take the blame for all of this! I may have started the Shadow Club, but it took all of them to breathe new life into it. I reasoned that if I still held some mysterious power over this club, now was the time to wield it.

I went straight up to Brett. "I started the Shadow Club, and I ended it," I said. "Take that stupid hat off your head." I reached up and swatted off the hat, and in turn he hit me, knocking me across the boat. It rocked slightly in its cradle as I hit the side.

"We don't *really* need you," he said. He grabbed me again and threw me across to the other side of the boat. Everyone shifted out of the way of our fight. "Are you beginning to get the picture?"

My answer was a punch to his jaw. It stunned him, but not enough. He grabbed me again and hurled me to the other side of the boat.

Then the world began to move.

Metal fatigue. That's what they call it when a piece of hardware gives way and something big comes tumbling down, usually taking a whole lot of lives with it. With all those kids jammed into the hull of the old tugboat, some-thing was bound to give. I heard the wood creak, and somewhere a piece of metal snapped, falling to the ground with a muted *clang*. Then the rusted steel cradle that held the tugboat gave way, and with a crash of metal, the entire ship fell to one side.

I've never been in an earthquake, but I imagine that's what it feels like, because thirty kids were hurled off their feet as the tugboat rocked to the right, then to the left, coming to rest. No one was screaming. People don't really scream in a real emergency—not unless they have a good long time to think about what is going to happen to them. There were just a few gasps and groans as kids hit the bulkhead. Funny thing about being in the hull of a ship that's tilted over on its side—you can't tell which way is down. It was strange enough with the floor tilting up like a V from the center, but now, with the ship fallen over on its side, my equilibrium was all thrown off. When I tried to stand up I just fell over as if I was drunk.

Everyone tried to gather themselves back together, wondering what had happened, but I already knew. The boat was resting in such a way that the hole in the hull—the one we all climbed through—*should* have been flat against the concrete now, leaving no way to get out. But instead there was light pouring through the hole—in fact, more light than before.

"Nobody move," I shouted, and for an instant everybody actually listened to me. We might have made it out had it not been for Brett. He was behind me, next to Alec, but he pushed me out of the way and made a beeline toward the hole in the hull, hurling kids out of the way in his panic to escape. When he finally reached the hole at the back of the boat, he jumped out and disappeared, falling like a paratrooper out of a plane. Then came his surprised distant yell, suddenly silenced by a *splash* that told me what I already suspected:

When the boat cradle gave way and the tug had fallen out, the tug's back end had slid over the edge of the seawall. There was no telling how close the entire tug was to slipping off the ledge and into the sea.

"Nobody move!" I screamed again, but Brett had already opened the door to panic. Now, having had enough time to think about their predicament, kids began to scream and jump over one another, racing for that little hole.

"Don't!" I yelled. "Don't you get it? We have to stay toward the front or—"

The boards creaked as the boat slid a little farther. Still they were crowding the hole, dropping through, one by one, into the water of the marina, figuring it was better than being trapped in the boat. It was like thirty people trying to escape from an elevator that was about to plunge.

I suppose I was in a panic, too, because I froze, not knowing what to do. But the thing about this I will always remember is that *Tyson* had the presence of mind to see the whole picture. He grabbed me by the shoulders to get my attention.

"Untie Alec," he said, looking me straight in the eye.

His look said everything. It gave me the whole picture, and the picture was this: with everyone shifting the weight of the precariously balanced tug, nothing we could do would stop it from going over the edge—which meant that things were about to get a whole lot worse. If we didn't untie Alec now, it might be the last chance we got.

And so, as the other kids crowded the hole, Tyson and I got behind Alec and worked the ropes. Luckily for us they weren't exactly seamen's knots. A little bit of tugging and they came undone. Alec didn't have much energy left, but he did dredge up enough to groan and complain at us all the while, still only seeing his own predicament and not the greater danger. Just about the instant the last knot came undone and Alec pulled his hands and feet free, the boat listed more on its side, giving off that sickly creaking of wood.

"Brace!" I said, grabbing onto the post that Alec had been tied to. The light through the hole changed, the world tilted, and gravity took over. My mind was filled with the strange surreal sight of twenty kids floating weightless in the hollow hull of a boat. Time seemed to dilate for that horrible instant, then everyone was smashed back down as the tug hit the water.

I was torn from the post. My shoulder hit a rib of the

hull, not hard enough to break, but hard enough to leave a deep bruise, assuming I survived to have a bruise. There was no light coming through the hole in the boat now, only water gushing in like a geyser. In seconds, the back end of the boat was filling up with water. The only light now came from various flashlights the kids had held, all of which were now scattered on the ground, aiming in random directions. I grabbed one and shone it into the faces scurrying up from the stern of the boat. How many kids could I count? How many had gotten out before the boat fell? What if someone was knocked unconscious by the fall and was still down there in the stern—or even worse, what if kids who were already out in the water were hit by the falling tugboat? There was no way to know.

A single ladder at the tugboat's widest point went up to a closed hatch, which I assumed led up to the main deck of the tug.

"This way," I shouted, pointing the light at the ladder. When I shone the flashlight back at them, the water level was higher. The entire stern was underwater now. Those kids farthest away were treading water and it was already beginning to pool around my feet, soaking through my sneakers. Then came that horrid creaking of wood again as the boat shifted from its side back to center, forcing the stern to sink even deeper. The few kids that hadn't screamed yet were screaming now.

The first kids reached the ladder and began scrambling up.

"One at a time," I yelled, but, of course, it was no use. When panic sets in, common sense is always the first casualty. They were on top of one another, tugging at each other, fighting to get up the ladder just as they had fought to get out of the hole before the boat fell. The first kid to the top of the ladder pushed on the hatch, but it didn't give.

"It won't open!" he screamed. "It's nailed shut. It's nailed shut and we're all going to drown!"

"Hit it again!" I told him. "Harder this time!"

When he hit it, the wood rattled enough for me to know that it wasn't nailed shut. It might have been locked from above, but like everything else in this old vessel, the lock would have rusted into nothing after years of salty air.

There were three kids up there now, all clinging to an edge of the ladder, pushing at the hatch with their arms and with their shoulders. Finally the hatch broke and flung open, letting in that wonderful light of day. The water was up to my knees now, and the flooding hull got dimmer and dimmer as more and more flashlights submerged and shorted out. Once it was open, those kids on the ladder didn't look back; they went out through the hole and the rest began to follow.

The water was up to my waist and rising fast—I could see it spilling in from between the weak, rotten boards of the hull, and still there were more than a dozen kids to get out.

None of them looked at me as they passed, they just kept their eyes fixed on that ladder and freedom. All the while, Tyson stood next to me, one hand on the ladder, the other grabbing floundering kids, helping them to the ladder. The last one to go was that chess-team girl—the one who had been so anxious for me "to get back at Alec."

"Checkmate" I wanted to say, but I didn't. Instead I just pushed her up toward the ladder, and she grabbed the rungs.

The water was up to my chest now, and that's when the cold really hit me. I could feel my muscles knotting, balling up in shock. I thought the ocean was cold in October when I had taken the plunge and saved Tyson, but that was nothing compared to this.

When all the others were gone, and Tyson and I were ready to go up the ladder, something occurred to me with a sense of dread that was sinking faster than the ship.

I hadn't seen Alec on the ladder.

I told Tyson, and he hesitated for a second. The water rose past my armpits.

"He must have gone up. Right? We got everybody out. He must have gone up."

"One of us would have seen him."

I wasted no time and did a surface dive, swimming as far down as I could go in that sunken hull, but even with the flashlight I couldn't see anything clearly in that murky water. I found nothing but loose timber, dead flashlights, hats—so many hats—then my own flashlight shorted out, leaving me in darkness.

I was at the end of my breath, and I realized I hadn't saved enough air to make it back to the ladder. With my chest aching and my head pounding, I swam forward, but when I got to where I thought the ladder was, I came up, bumping my head against a crossbeam, and I was still underwater.

The air is gone, I thought. The boat is entirely underwater now. How deep was the marina? How far down would the boat sink? And if I did find the hatch now, how far would I have to swim to reach the surface? Twenty feet? A hundred? With my lungs ready to explode, I propelled myself forward, my head still bumping against wood, then finally I surfaced into a pitch-black space. Coughing, sputtering, gasping deep breaths of air, I tried to get my bearings. I had no idea where I was, but as my breathing came under control, I heard just to my right someone else breathing.

"Alec?"

"Leave me alone!" His voice came through what must have been clenched teeth. I knew, because I was clenching my teeth to keep from shivering my fillings out. Now I had felt around enough to get a good idea where we were. We were in an air pocket at the very tip of the bow.

"Come on, the hatch is only about ten feet back," I told him. "We can make it, easy."

"Fine. You can go," Alec said.

Now, considering the fact that I was freezing and scared out of my mind, I was in no mood to deal with a pouting five-year-old, which was exactly how Alec sounded.

"Alec!"

"You wanna know why we moved here?" Alec said. "You wanna know why?"

"Alec, this really isn't the time for some deep, personal conversation, OK?"

"It's because they hated me there, too. We moved here so I could get a fresh start in a place where all the other kids didn't hate me."

"Not everyone hates you—just half of everyone." I couldn't believe I was being dragged into this. "Can't you just shut up long enough to save your own hide?"

"I hope they all drown," he said. "Every last one of them."

"No you don't—and don't even *think* it, because if any of them do drown, you'll never forgive yourself for thinking that."

"If *they* don't drown," Alec said, "maybe *I* should."

There was a splash next to me, I felt something brush past me, and for a bizarre moment my mind filled with the image of a shark—but instead someone surfaced and began taking deep breaths.

"Jared," said Tyson, struggling to clear the water from his

lungs. "I felt you swim past me before. You missed the hatch."

"Tell me something I don't know."

"I'm going to kill you for not teaching me how to swim underwater," Tyson said.

"I was going to get to it, eventually," I told him. "Alec's here, too." I moved over and bumped my head against an iron crossbeam that felt uneasily loose.

"So, are we just going to sit here and drown ourselves? Is that the plan?" Tyson asked.

"Alec's feeling sorry for himself," I informed Tyson. "Says he wants to die."

I could hear Tyson's teeth chattering now. "He might get his wish."

Just then I felt the boat hit bottom, shifting again. The jolt shook loose the crossbeam. It came plunging down, clipping my shoulder. I heard Alec yelp as he was struck and forced under by the weight of the beam. Suddenly the water that was just below my neck was up to my chin.

"Tyson!" I called.

"I'm OK," he said. "But Alec—"

"Alec!" I called. No answer. "Alec." But my voice was silenced as the last of the air emptied from the air pocket, and the old tugboat shuddered as it finally gave up the ghost.

Dead Reckoning

I WISH I could say that Tyson and I performed a heroic underwater rescue and saved Alec's life . . . but I can't.

As for the tugboat, its fall to the ocean deep wasn't exactly of *Titanic* proportions—in fact, the hatch was only a few feet underwater, and the tug's pilothouse still poked out of the bay like the conning tower of a submarine. But you see, it doesn't matter how much water there is; people can drown in one foot of water as easily as they can drown in a hundred feet.

I came up through the hatch, surprised by the short distance I had to rise until breaking the surface. My eyes quickly adjusted to the light, and when I looked around, I could see that the other kids had already made it to safety. Now they all clung to the edge of a dock no more than twenty yards away. They looked like a wet pack of stray dogs.

"We need help!" I screamed to them. "Alec's still underwater! He's pinned under a beam. I think . . . I think he might be dead."

Nobody moved—not a single one of them. I was furious, but not entirely surprised. Having just gotten off the tug with their lives, death had just been close enough without them having to haul it out from the depths.

Brett was the first to speak.

"The suction!" Brett yelled, clinging to a piling like a barnacle. "We got to stay away on account of the suction when it goes down."

"It's already sitting on the bottom, you idiot!"

Still we received no help, and Tyson—well, being the weak swimmer he was, it was all he could do just to tread water and stay afloat.

Cold as it was, I took a few deep breaths and went back down the hatch alone. My lungs held out as long as they needed to—a minute, maybe more. Then I surfaced, and the others watched as I came out from behind the pilothouse of the tug. Tyson, who had waited for me, labored to dog-paddle himself to the dock. I, on the other hand, had a much more grim task. With my arm across his chest, I pulled the limp, lifeless Alec in a slow, cross-chest carry toward the dock—just as I had done to Tyson four months before. Only this time, there was no fighting or kicking or struggling. Alec was a dead weight, putting up no fight at all. When I got halfway there, a few others jumped into the water to help me. We hauled him up onto the dock. I never knew a human body could be so heavy, so awkward. We let him go, and his head hit the wood with a *thud*. Water spilled from Alec's mouth. His lips were blue. His eyes half open. I don't know if any of the kids had ever seen a dead body before, but if they had, it was in much saner circumstances, in a funeral parlor surrounded by flowers and organ music. Half the kids there stared in disbelief; the other half looked away, unable to face what they saw. I labored to give him mouth-to-mouth, but nothing made any difference. Finally I stepped back from him and turned to the kids shivering around me.

"You got what you wanted," I said to the water-logged members of the new Shadow Club. "Alec Smartz won't be bothering anyone anymore."

No one said a thing. Brett looked as if he might pass out, stumbling for an instant, then he turned and he ran off the dock as fast as his legs could carry him, and kept on going.

"We're sorry," said Tommy Nickols. He'd been the ninth grade's best student until Alec came along. "We're so, so sorry—"

"Sorry?" I said. My voice growing louder as I spoke. "Tell his parents. Maybe it'll make them feel better, you think?" I couldn't tell whether the moistness in his eyes was tears, or just seawater. "You're gonna feel sorry for the rest of your life—all of you—and you know what? The feeling only gets worse."

Tommy finally burst into tears. "I'm sorry," he said. "Sorry, sorry, sorry."

By now Tyson had climbed up onto the dock as well and was catching his breath, his gaze fixed on Alec. "Someone ought to close his eyes," Tyson said. "It's not right leaving them open like that."

I looked around until I found the one girl who seemed to be trying to hide behind all the other kids, trying to be just a spectator and not a culprit.

"Jodi, you get yourself over here," I demanded. "Close his eyes."

"No," she said sheepishly. "You can do it."

"You owe it to him, Jodi," said Tyson, with more conviction in his voice than I had ever heard. "You do it, or nobody here will ever forgive you."

With that kind of pressure, Jodi finally came forward. The other kids parted for her, as if she had suddenly become an untouchable. With everyone watching, she knelt down in front of Alec's body. There were other kids crying now—some sobbing, others sniffling quietly. Jodi looked around one last time, hoping there was someone who would give her a last-minute reprieve from having to do this, but no one would. So, on her knees, she reached forward with two fingers spread like a peace sign toward Alec Smartz's half-opened eyes. Then, just as she was about to touch his lids, Alec said:

"Get out of my face."

If ever in the history of our town there was a Kodak moment, this was it. Jodi shrieked, and the skin on her face seemed to peel back as if she was under fighter-jet G-forces. She stumbled backward with the shock and fell on to the wet dock with a *splash* and a *thump*, receiving what I hoped was a whole constellation of splinters in her rear.

Like I said, I wish I could say that Tyson and I performed a heroic underwater rescue and saved Alec's life, but I can't. Because Alec didn't need saving. Like everything else, he was good at swimming. He had been hit by the falling cross-beam, but freed himself, and when the last of the air was forced from the air pocket, he was the first one out of the hatch. But I had a brainstorm on the way out—a brainstorm that turned Alec into a much-needed silver bullet; the very silver bullet we needed to deal a mortal blow to that monster called the Shadow Club. Alec was more than happy to play his part, because he got all the benefits of dying without actually having to go through with it.

He had hid in the tugboat's pilothouse when I went back down the hatch. The hardest part for him had to be not blinking and not flinching when his head hit the dock. I swear, for a moment there even I thought he was dead.

"That's not funny," said the chess-team girl, as Alec stood.

"It wasn't supposed to be funny," I told her.

Jodi got to her feet. "You're sick," Jodi said. "Both of you."

I had to laugh at that, but the laugh quickly faded. She actually thought *we* were the sick ones.

"You think your twisted little joke makes any difference?" she said. "The Shadow Club still has plenty of things left to do."

But I shook my head. "The Shadow Club is dead," I told her.

She looked around, unsure of her own support and, facing each other, we drew our lines in the sand as well as one could on a wooden dock.

"How many of you think the Shadow Club is dead?" I asked.

It was like a trick question in math class. Everyone looked to one another, no one wanted to make the first move, but Tommy Nickols, who was quite often the first to get any right answer, stepped forward. Then came another and another, until it became an entire mob moving over to stand beside Alec, Tyson, and me. I can't say Jodi was left alone—she wasn't. There were five or six kids who still stood beside her. I suppose there would always be those kids who found hate too tasty a flavor to give up. But the others—well, let's just say they lost their appetite.

Jodi broke off her cold eye contact with me and turned to Tyson, softening up a bit. "You don't owe him anything, Tyson," she told him. "You don't have to pretend to be on his side."

Tyson shrugged. "And just because we *were* going out doesn't mean I have to pretend to be on yours."

The police arrived quietly on the hill, no sirens, no rush. It was a single cruiser probably sent to investigate a call from a hillside neighbor who claimed boats were falling from the sky on this cold Presidents' Day. By the time they saw us, half the kids had run off—including Jodi—and the ones that remained were ready to confess whatever deeds they had done. These weren't the ones who needed to talk to the police, however. They needed to talk to their own parents. They needed to talk to Mr. Greene—to stand in his ruined house and confess to him. If we brought the police in now, we'd have nothing but hard feelings and headlines. Neither would do these kids any good.

I really did want to nail Jodi Lattimer to the wall for what she had done, but as the officers approached, I knew there was no chance of that.

"Jared Mercer," Deputy Lattimer said. "I should have known." He looked at the bunch of kids who were trying hard not to shiver. "What happened here?"

"The tugboat fell," I told him. "The wind blew it loose. We saw it fall."

"How come you're all wet?"

"Polar Bear Club," Alec quickly answered. "We read about them in the news—you know, people who go swimming in the middle of winter. We thought we'd try it."

"It sucked," added Tyson.

Deputy Lattimer studied Tyson for a moment. "Haven't I seen you with my daughter?"

"It won't happen again."

"Good."

He asked a few more questions, but in the end, he took the whole thing at face value. We were just a bunch of kids doing something stupid on Presidents' Day. I know I should have felt bad looking him in the eye and telling him something completely untrue, but I had been a good kid and I had been a bad kid, and both had taught me a thing or two. Such as "honesty is the best policy," except when it's best to lie. Having seen firsthand the lengths to which parents will go to protect their children, I knew this was not the time or place for the truth about his daughter.

He offered to shuttle us all home, but there were few takers, as it was better to be cold and wet than show up at home in a police car.

Once he had gone, the rest of us left for warmer places, no one talking as we made our separate ways home. I lingered with Tyson and Alec for a little, taking some shelter from the wind behind a boarded-up tackle shop.

"Did you really have to give me mouth-to-mouth?" Alec asked.

I cringed at the memory. "I had to make it look realistic. Believe me, it was no great pleasure."

Tyson held his arms across his chest as a gust of wind added to our chill. "You think your mom will have something good for dinner?" Tyson asked.

I laughed. To my mom even Thanksgiving came out of a box, and today was only Presidents' Day. "What do *you* think?"

Tyson sighed. "Probably pizza or takeout."

I turned to look at what was left of the tugboat. Its pilothouse was still above water, but I knew it would completely submerge, come high tide.

Then I looked at Alec, still swollen from the beating he had suffered. What do you say to a kid who, two hours ago tried to kill you, then almost got killed himself? "You wanna come home with us, Alec?" I asked. "Hang for a while?"

"Not really," he said. But he was soaked, the wind was still blowing, and as he looked up the road, I could tell he was thinking how much farther away his home was than mine.

"Sure, maybe for a while," he said.

Because sometimes it's like they say, "Any port in a storm."

Random Acts of Violets

MY ALARM WENT went off the next morning, chirping its evil shrill call, and after I hit the snooze button half a dozen times, Mom came to roust me out of bed. I rose to a typical morning—the only hint that anything out of the ordinary had happened were the bruises and muscle aches I had earned the day before.

Tyson was already at the breakfast table, inhaling a bowl of Corn Pops. Dad was mumbling to himself in his standard ritual of searching for his misplaced car keys.

After what happened, you'd think the world would just stop on its axis, but Tuesday came with such dull normality, it was enough to make a person sick. The sun, at least, had the common courtesy to hide its face behind a blanket of clouds for most of the day.

School wasn't much different; classes rolled at their typical snail's pace, and although I saw many of the kids who had been there the day before, none of us made eye contact.

I stopped by Mr. Greene's office before second period. I didn't know quite what to tell him. He deserved to know the whole story, but I wasn't up to reliving it. By the look of him, he wasn't up to it either. He looked older today. Well, maybe not older, but a bit more world-weary, as if his body and spirit no longer felt like fighting gravity. I wondered if I had that look, too.

"You'll be happy to know that the Shadow Club finally took a silver bullet, chased with a stake through the heart."

Mr. Greene eyed me with a suspicious mix of emotions. Then he said, "Brett Whatley has disappeared. Does that have anything to do with your silver bullet?"

"Yes, and no," I told him. "Brett ran off when he found out he had killed Alec Smartz."

Greene showed confusion, rather than shock. "But I just saw Alec a minute ago—"

"Exactly."

Greene stepped forward, about to ask something, but took a deep breath, reigning in his own curiosity. "Thank you," he said. "You'd better go, or you'll be late for class."

I turned and headed for the door, but just before I left he said, "Be vigilant, Jared."

I turned back to him. "Excuse me?"

"Stakes and silver bullets don't always take," he said. "Be vigilant."

I left, closing the door quietly, taking with me an uneasy vertigo left by Greene's advice.

The next day Brett Whatley stumbled out of the woods two towns away and headed straight for the nearest police department, where he tearfully confessed to having killed Alec Smartz.

When they called the Smartz home to inform the parents of this awful crime, Alec answered the phone, casting serious doubt on Brett's claim.

"Brett just kept sobbing and sobbing," Alec told me. "He couldn't believe I was alive. He didn't even ask how. 'You're the best, Alec,' he says, 'I love ya, man!'"

"He actually said 'I love ya, man'?"

"Swear to God—and then he tells me he's my slave for life."

"You gonna take him up on it?" I asked.

"I don't know. Maybe just long enough to have him clean out our garage."

Apparently our silver bullet had pierced Brett's brain and turned him into a repentant puppy. I knew it would set the mood for the other club members as well, but I wasn't satisfied. There was still more to do.

Mr. Greene had been right—killing the Shadow Club wasn't good enough—because then it would become legend, the way it had before. Its memory would loom larger than life, enticing others to invoke it again. No, the Shadow Club needed a different fate. That's why I went to the mall and ordered a whole bunch of denim caps to replace the ones lost at sea in the tugboat plunge. In school I found each of the kids who had been there and shoved a hat into their hands, telling them exactly what I expected them to do and exactly when I expected them to do it. And although none of them wanted any part of it, many of them reluctantly took the hats and agreed. That's how I found myself the leader of the Shadow Club again.

The following Saturday morning, the bitterly widowed and lately deflowered Hilda McBroom awoke to a commotion on her lawn. What she found was a whole bunch of kids wreaking havoc in her recently murdered garden. She stormed outside, cordless phone in hand, no doubt ready to call 911, which she probably had on auto dial.

"Who are you kids? What are you doing here? Haven't you made enough mischief yet? What else do you want from me, blood?"

I stepped forward. "That's a lot of questions, Mrs. McBroom."

She wagged an arthritic finger at me. "I know you! You're that Mercer boy, aren't you? The one who caused all that trouble!" She turned to Cheryl. "And you! You're that Gannett girl—you're just as bad as him."

"We understand you've been having some problems with your garden," Cheryl said.

I pointed to my hat. Denim, with the letters TSC in bright orange across the face. "We're the Tree and Shrub Crew," I told her. "No garden goes unplanted. That's our motto."

Moose SanGiorgio rolled up with a wheelbarrow overloaded with winter-clipped rosebushes. "Hi, Old Lady. Where do you want these?"

"Leave my garden alone," she said. "I don't want any Tree and Shrub Crew!"

"Tough luck," shouted Brett Whatley from across the yard, "because you've got us, whether you like it or not." Brett's offer of perpetual servitude had apparently extended beyond just Alec. He didn't just turn over a new leaf, he flipped that sucker and pinned it for the count. Although he no longer dared to claim any leadership position, his take-my-help-and-love-it attitude helped to define us now.

There were more than twenty kids working away in Mrs. McBroom's garden. Many were members of the new Shadow Club—but the club's original members were there, too. Darren, Abbie, O. P., all of them. The new members showed up to redeem their guilt, and the originals showed up because I asked them. Of course the originals had complained.

"Why do *we* have to do it?" Jason had said. "*We* didn't do anything bad this time."

So I told them they didn't have to come, but I'd like it if they did. I guess I must still carry some clout, because they all showed up.

As for the rosebushes, they came from our own yards, along with other flowering shrubs that would bloom a full spectrum of color, come spring. If any of our parents were annoyed by it, once they knew where the plants were going, they kept their complaints and their questions to themselves.

Mrs. McBroom paced on her porch with a combination of disbelief and horror as she watched us replant her garden, threatening every five minutes to call the police, until finally she gave up and came out to direct us, telling us exactly where she wanted each plant to go.

Solerno's stayed closed for two weeks. According to Old Man Solerno, he would never set foot in the place again. His days as a restauranteur had come to an end. Naturally, when the place came back to life the next Sunday afternoon, Solerno was furious. Tipped off by an anonymous phone call, he arrived at his restaurant to find about two dozen kids making an absolute mess in his kitchen.

Like Mrs. McBroom, he threatened to call the police on us. Like Mrs. McBroom, he never actually dialed. Under protest, he sat down at one of his own tables, and we served him about fifteen different dishes—our parents' favorite

Italian recipes, which we had practiced cooking at home. "What's-a this all about?" Solerno asked, almost afraid to try the food.

"We're The Solerno Committee," I told him, pointing to the initials on my hat. "Your food stinks, so we thought we'd change your menu and convince you to open up again. After all, this town wouldn't be the same without Solerno's."

He called me a lousy rotten punk and crossed his arms as plate after plate was set before him. Finally the aroma of fresh garlic and basil weakened him, and he tried one dish. We must have done a good job, because he moved on from the first plate to the second to the third, sampling them all. Some of them he tried three and four times. Finally he separated them into two categories. He pointed to the ones to his left. "I add-a these to my menu, eh?" Then he pointed to the ones to his right. "These other ones, they make-a me puke."

He tasted the ones he liked once more. "Need-a more salt," he said.

The next Wednesday morning, five of the pudgier members of the Shadow Club went knocking on Garson Underwood's door just as he was about to leave for his morning jog. According to their report, here's how it went:

"We're here to go jogging with you," they told him.

He laughed, thinking it was some sort of joke, but when they didn't leave, he began to wonder what was going on.

"We want to get into shape," one of them said. "And since we knew you jog every day, we thought we could jog with you. Because, as you can see from our hats we're Tired of Sitting on the Couch."

From what I heard, he was distrustful of the whole thing—what with vandals in town destroying his car—but he must have sensed some sincerity in the kids, because he took them with him on his morning jog. At last report, he still jogs with them every morning, and has taken to wearing his own TSC hat, because he, too, is Tired of Sitting on the Couch.

Pretty soon word began to get out that some creepy bunch of juvenile philanthropists were making the rounds in town, striking when least expected. It was sort of good-deed terrorism, dumped on unsuspecting victims whether they wanted it or not. I figured if the Shadow Club was only capable of acts of aggression, why couldn't those acts be aggressively good? No one seemed to make the connection that these were the same kids who had caused the trouble a couple of weeks before. I guess it's true that once people see you in one light, it's hard for them to see you in another. This time it worked to our advantage.

"When is it going to stop?" Cheryl asked.

"I hope it doesn't," I told her.

There were still a hundred things left to do. Solerno's and Broom Hilda's garden were just drops in the bucket, but that was all right. Hatred and violence, I knew, could be habit forming—but so could acts of kindness—and just because the Shadow Club had its origins in small-town terrorism didn't mean it couldn't redefine itself. It took vision. It took *vigilance*, as Mr. Greene had said—never turning a blind eye, always being aware of the danger. Vigilance not just for today, but tomorrow, and every day after that. A long-term goal.

Me, I've always been a goal-oriented person, the finish line always in my sights. True, I had always been a sprinter, but perhaps it was time to become a distance runner. If I could pace myself, I knew I could pace all of them—all of *us*—who wore the hat. It wasn't exactly a Boy Scout hat, if you know what I mean—there was still quite a lot of Shaditude in the things we did—and that seemed to satisfy even the angriest outsiders who had gravitated to the group. But we couldn't reach everyone. And I knew that *those* were the ones to be careful of.

That's why I mailed the package.

I had wrapped the package, and it sat on my desk for days before I decided to actually mail it.

"What's that?" Tyson asked, stepping into my room. "A letter bomb?"

"Thermonuclear," I told him, handing it to him.

"Amazing how small those things are getting." He

looked it over, then tossed the small package back to me. "Do me a favor, don't detonate it tonight. I'm taking Marla Nixbok to the Gazilliaplex."

"Fine, I promise not to smash your atoms before *she* does." And then I laughed. "*Marla Nixbok Dates Tyson McGaw*—isn't that one of the biblical signs of the end of the world?"

"Ha-ha," he said. "You just can't stand that I'm not a freak anymore."

"You were never a freak," I told him with deep sincerity. "Just a loser." I thought he might curse me out, but instead he just smiled, and I smiled back. "Have a good time, Tyson," I told him, and added, "Don't kiss her with popcorn in your mouth. That grosses girls out."

He laughed. "Can I write that down? My first bit of brotherly advice."

Brotherly. Now, *there* was a thermonuclear word.

"So . . . I guess my parents talked to you about it," I said cautiously. "They told me they would."

Tyson looked away. "They mentioned it. They said it's up to me."

"So, what do you think?"

Tyson shrugged, for a brief moment looking like the scared kid I once rescued from his own flames. "I'm not sure yet. I mean, my initials would be the same, right? But calling myself Tyson Mercer would be weird. Still, I wouldn't mind it, y'know? Being your brother?" He thought about it a moment more, then brightened. "Tell you what. When I decide, you'll be the first to know."

"Fair enough."

After he left, I returned my attention to the small package that still had no address. If it was a letter bomb, it wasn't much of one, but it wasn't a large-scale type of thing. It was more like a surgical strike. Carefully I wrote the address in block letters. Then I took a run down to the post office, getting there just before it closed.

There have been a lot of changes in my life over the past year—awful things I've seen and done, mistakes I've made. A person can grow from mistakes, or a person can deny them completely, letting their anger build up inside them until it blows. That's why I sent my little letter bomb.

And so, tomorrow or the next day, Jodi Lattimer will receive a package. It will have no return address, no hint of who sent it, but she'll know all the same. Because she will open it to find—wrapped in tissue paper—a shiny seashell, about the size of her fist. I don't know what she'll hear when she holds it up to her ear, but maybe, just maybe she'll hear the echoes of the world around her and finally feel the depth of the pain she helped to cause.

But if, in the end, all she can hear is the sea . . . then vigilance will have to be enough.